MANGO

A LOVE BEYOND BOUNDARIES

KOKI LOGAN

INDIA · SINGAPORE · MALAYSIA

ISBN 979-8-89026-363-6

Introducing "Monsoon Tango: A Love Beyond Boundaries" - a captivating and persuasive tale that takes you on a rollercoaster ride of friendship, love, and resilience, inspired by real-life incidents.

Set against the backdrop of a prestigious university in the United States, this heartwarming story revolves around the deep bond shared between Abhi Kumar, an Indian student, and Robi Bascom, an African American student. Their friendship defies cultural barriers and spans continents, forming the bedrock of a remarkable journey filled with triumphs and tribulations.

As the inseparable duo embarks on a series of adventures, they decide to venture into the world of business in India, defying conventional paths and embracing the unknown. Together, they navigate the intricate tapestry of entrepreneurship, shaping their destinies while experiencing the vibrant tapestry of Indian culture.

Amidst their journey, love takes center stage when Robi finds himself irresistibly drawn to Gayatri, Abhi's enchanting cousin sister. However, their blossoming romance is met with staunch resistance in the culturally conservative setting they find themselves in. With hearts broken and friendships strained, the obstacles they face seem insurmountable.

But love knows no boundaries, and the indomitable spirit of the protagonists shines through as they confront their deepest fears and fight against the odds. Their journey takes them on a sensational path, traversing continents once again, as they strive to unite against all odds. The remarkable embodiment of love becomes their guiding light, inspiring them to overcome every obstacle in their path.

"Monsoon Tango: A Love Beyond Boundaries" is a work of fiction that celebrates the power of love, friendship, and the human spirit. It serves as a testament to the resilience and determination that fuels our souls, urging us to defy societal norms and embrace the extraordinary. Prepare to be enthralled as you witness the transformative journey of Abhi, Robi, and Gayatri, and discover the true meaning of love that transcends all boundaries.

Contents

Part III: California, USA

Author's Note

Embarking on the journey of penning this novel has proven to be an ambitious undertaking, one that involved traversing continents and dedicating considerable time to its completion. As a work of fiction, I have intertwined real-life incidents and locations to establish a profound connection between the readers and the story. Throughout the process, I had the privilege of writing in the very locations where the narrative unfolded, immersing myself in the authentic ambiance and essence of each place. While it may not be a common practice among established writers, I felt compelled to personally visit and experience the key locations mentioned in the book.

Above all, my intention was to create a feel-good novel that celebrates the essence of true friendship and evokes a sense of old-style romance, transcending geographical boundaries and igniting genuine emotions that nourish the soul. It was a heartfelt endeavor to craft a story that would leave a lasting impression on the hearts of readers, reminding them of the beauty and significance of meaningful relationships.

The global pandemic, which brought about a complete travel ban and an unprecedented level of uncertainty, paradoxically facilitated the completion and refinement of this novel. For approximately seven months, my family found themselves scattered across four continents, leaving me grappling with immense stress and uncertainty. In this trying period, writing became my sole means of expression, providing solace and purpose.

I wholeheartedly attribute the completion of this endeavor to my wonderful wife, who provided timely inputs, motivation, and patiently did the final editing of the document. I also want to express my gratitude to my lovely kids, who beamed with pride and encouraged me when I revealed that I was writing the book.

Last but not the least, thanks to my dedicated publishing team at Notion Press, who made this a reality!

Part I: California, USA

Chapter 1

Bon Voyage

The sultry and unbearable Chennai weather lingered, even past 8 o'clock in the evening. August's monsoon season intensified the heat, but it didn't deter the influx of people from various parts of India and the world to the captivating city. Chennai had an undeniable allure.

On a humid August evening in 2006, Abhishek Kumar, known as Abhi, embarked on a journey abroad via Chennai International Airport, leaving behind his native city for the next two years. Abhi, accompanied by his parents, Kumar and Malini, and his cousin sister Gayatri, rode in the family Innova car. They were joined by a procession of five other cars carrying close relatives and friends bidding Abhi farewell on his voyage to the United States.

After weeks of hectic preparation, Abhi mentally prepared himself for his new life as a student at the prestigious Stanford University in California. He had been accepted into the Master's in Engineering Economics program. However, in that moment, he was caught up in the present, feeling an unusual silence within the car. His Blackberry overflowed with SMS wishes and flowery emails, while his Skype and other chat accounts brimmed with messages from friends and well-wishers. Abhi had a vast network of supporters, and he knew he would miss them.

The deafening silence persisted until Abhi's mother, Malini, broke the ice in her usual motherly fashion. "Abhi-Kanna, make sure you rest properly and eat on time. If you don't like the dorm food, have the instant meal packets kept in your suitcases. And be cautious when eating outside with your university friends."

Abhi smiled and reassured her, "Amma, relax! I'll be fine. The San Francisco Bay Area is just as good as Chennai. Everything is available there. Remember our vacation to Los Angeles? We had the best food there. San Francisco Bay Area is even better."

"Okay, okay. Be brave, study well, come back, get married, and settle down," Malini said with a contorted smile, a perfected expression only mothers possess.

Gayatri smiled at her cousin, playfully nudging him. As expected, Abhi responded, "Amma, relax now. I'll let you know when I'm ready. Why are you bringing up these things so early in my life? Let me be myself for some time."

Now it was Abhi's father, Kumar's, turn to offer some wisdom. "Alright, Abhi. Remember to keep your passport, tickets, and boarding pass safe at all times, especially during security checks. You should recall a few things from our vacation a few years ago. Give us a call as soon as you reach San Francisco, and keep the university contact numbers handy. They've arranged a ride for you at the airport."

After a brief pause, Kumar continued, "Once you settle into your apartment, open a bank account and get a credit card. Don't worry about finances; we'll fully support you. Focus on your studies, campus life, and form meaningful friendships. Also, we'll be available on Skype whenever you need to connect."

Abhi grew emotional at this point. The realization hit him that he would spend a considerable amount of time away from his family. He anticipated more emotional triggers ahead, including bouts of homesickness.

As always in Chennai, rain and thunderstorms suddenly unleashed their fury. Abhi's family driver Vetrivel, who is affectionately known as Vetri, skillfully navigated the chaos, bringing them to the departure area of Chennai International Airport. The usual commotion made the airport feel more like a suburban railway station than a modern aviation hub.

Abhi and his father stepped out of the car, carrying the heavy luggage that would accompany him to the States. Overwhelmed with emotions, Abhi struggled to process his father's words. Finally, it sank in that his father was once again advising him to be careful with his passport, tickets, and wallet, stressing the importance of keeping everything intact during security checks.

Abhi's mother and Gayatri followed the men, bidding their favorite person farewell. Abhi decided to wait for the entire entourage to arrive. About twenty of them gathered near the departure gate, each offering a heartfelt hug and emotionally charged bon voyage to their beloved "Abhi."

At this juncture, Abhi was overcome with tears, and his parents and Gayatri were also deeply moved. The emotionally charged farewell etched an enduring memory in his mind.

Since visitors were not allowed beyond the departure gate, Abhi took a few extra minutes to be with his loved ones and friends before waving goodbye to everyone. In a dazed and highly emotional state, Abhi checked in for his Singapore Airlines flight to San Francisco via Singapore and Seoul. While waiting to go through immigration and security, Abhi read through the text messages and emails on his Blackberry and made a few quick calls, but not fully present in the moment.

Around 10 PM, Abhi was called to board. He didn't mind the commotion caused by passengers rushing through the gate. With tears streaming down his face, he turned off his phone after making a final call to his parents and prepared for his solo trip to the land of "milk and honey."

Abhi wasn't savoring the moment as much as he should have. Leaving his cherished home for a couple of years proved to be challenging. The genial attendants on the flight directed him to his seat, where he felt slightly drowsy and dizzy from the intensity of the emotions and events.

He was now leaving his familiar territory, embarking on a journey to a new destination—perhaps the journey of a lifetime.

Chapter 2

Sky High Dreams: New Beginnings in San Francisco

Abhi found solace in the opportunity to catch some sleep during the first leg of his journey, which involved transits in Singapore and Seoul before reaching San Francisco. He mentally prepared himself for the long journey and embraced the upcoming odyssey that awaited him in a completely new environment. Although memories of his childhood and homesickness started creeping in, Abhi made a conscious effort not to let his emotions overwhelm him. Instead, he reflected positively on his upbringing in Chennai, cherishing memories of his loving parents, friends, and the experiences that shaped him.

To distract himself, Abhi took out a mini photo album from his carry-on bag. The album contained cherished photos from his baby days, reminding him of the love and affection bestowed upon him by his parents, grandparents, and friends. Abhi felt very fortunate to have been born as the only child to Kumar and Malini. However, he couldn't help but admit that he sometimes wished for a sibling. Nevertheless, his cousin sister, Gayatri, filled the void and provided all the affection and support.

Kumar, Abhi's father, came from a prominent South Indian business family that valued education. While they excelled in building businesses for generations, they also recognized the importance of obtaining degrees abroad. Despite their traditional roots in Chennai, the family embraced global changes. Kumar himself had completed his Bachelor's degree in engineering from the prestigious College of Engineering, Guindy, Chennai, and was ready to make his mark.

Malini, Abhi's mother, grew up in a traditional Tamil middle-class household that was home to lawyers, professors, doctors, collectors, and intellectuals. She met Kumar through Kumar's sister during her college days and was drawn to his caring and humble nature. Kumar, on the other hand, was captivated by Malini's warmth, grace, and her passion for singing and dancing. Surprisingly, both families found common ground and fully supported the union between Kumar and Malini. The couple got engaged and celebrated their grand wedding in 1982, after Kumar completed his Master's degree in the UK and joined the family business. Throughout their marriage, they remained committed to their vows of love, care, and family responsibilities. While Kumar dedicated himself to the family business, Malini pursued a part-time career in child psychology and education.

In April 1984, Abhi was born, bringing immense joy to Kumar and Malini. The family felt complete, and they named their son Abhishek after much deliberation. Abhi grew up in a harmonious environment, receiving equal love and attention from both his parents and their respective families.

Abhi's thoughts drifted back to his early days—his first birthday, his first day at school, and the countless memories of tennis at the club and partying with friends. His parents ensured that he had everything he needed without spoiling him, instilling in him a strong value system. Academically gifted, Abhi excelled effortlessly, but he also actively participated in extracurricular activities to develop into a well-rounded individual.

While growing up, Abhi embraced a traditional mindset, honoring family aspirations and traditions while enjoying the pleasures within those boundaries. He developed a strong and independent mindset that helped him prioritize his goals and aspirations in life. Despite his wealth and good looks, he never felt inclined to show off or indulge in excessive partying like some of his peers.

Abhi cherished the close bond he had with his cousin sister, Gayatri. They practically grew up together, attending the same school in Chennai, and their age difference of just two years made them inseparable. Abhi saw Gayatri as his baby sister and protected her fiercely. He took immense pride in her grace, demeanor, and intelligence, and she reciprocated his affection with unwavering support.

As the tedium of the long journey wore on, Abhi struggled to adjust. It had been a while since he had taken such a long transcontinental flight, and the layover in Singapore was longer than expected. Feeling like a zombie, he moved through airports, and the accompanying jet lag only added to his weariness. However, he looked forward to reaching one of the most beautiful places on Earth, San Francisco Bay Area, home to Stanford University—one of the most prestigious institutions in the United States.

Finally, the descent into the SFO airport began. The smooth touchdown and the bright sunshine lifted Abhi's spirits. He disembarked, bidding farewell to the hospitable crew that had served him throughout the long journey. Abhi was captivated by the multicultural atmosphere of the SFO international airport, realizing it was the ultimate destination for those seeking freedom and merit-based opportunities. The new environment had a relatively positive effect on him, and he felt neither intimidated nor overwhelmed by the sheer scale of everything around him.

While going through the immigration line, Abhi observed the diverse mix of people quietly proceeding to the passport control and immigration counters. When he reached the counter, a cheerful officer warmly greeted him. Skillfully examining Abhi's student visa paperwork, passport, and Stanford University credentials, the officer commented, "Stanford, huh? Good deal, brother! How long do you plan to stay in the US?"

Anticipating the question, Abhi confidently replied, "Thank you, Sir! Just about two years. I've promised my parents that I'll return once I finish my education and join the family business." It was the same response he had given to the US Consulate officer during his visa interview in Chennai.

The officer remarked, "Oh yeah! That's what everyone says, bro! But I see them here even after ten or twenty years." He playfully stamped Abhi's passport and visa paperwork, wishing him luck and a great time.

Nervously smiling back, Abhi walked out of the immigration area, finally setting foot in the United States and eagerly embracing the next phase of his student life. After collecting his bags, he breezed through customs without any inspections, approaching the entry door that marked the gateway to his new world.

Chapter 3

A Chance Encounter

Abhi felt a bit of excitement and a touch of apprehension as he entered the massive reception area of SFO International Airport. The bustling scene was filled with formal hugs, laughter, and instant photographs, where agents from companies or hotels welcomed new arrivals with placards or photographs. Instinctively, Abhi headed towards the information counter to dial the university number he had. However, before he could reach the counter, a tall and handsome African American gentleman with a placard displaying his name approached him.

"Are you Aabeesheikh? Headed towards Stanford?" the man asked.

"Yes, yes! I am Abhishek. Please call me Abhi," responded Abhi, feeling a wave of relief.

"Hey Abhi! I'm Robi, man! Welcome to America, or rather, sunny California! I'm your pick-up guy from Stanford. Your buddy, Rahul, did some sweet talkin' to get me to do this," Robi beamed, shaking Abhi's hand.

"Don't be nervous, Abhi! This is California, man! We're both students here. So, how was the flight, dude?" Robi asked.

"It was long and tiring, but I'm glad I made it Robi," responded Abhi with a smile.

Abhi found himself quickly warming up to Robi's friendly attitude. Robi took the luggage cart from him and urged him to follow to the parking lot, singing, jiving, and doing everything to cheer Abhi up as if they had been friends for years.

Abhi immediately sensed that Robi was genuinely kind and trying to make him feel at home. Riding the elevator a few levels up to the parking lot, Abhi appreciated Robi's help in pulling the heavy cart.

Robi owned a well-maintained mid-sized Toyota Camry, fairly new and in good condition. As they transferred the bags to the trunk, Robi couldn't resist asking, "Abhi, what's in these bags, dude? Looks like you're carrying enough goodies to feed the entire campus!"

Abhi chuckled and replied, "Oh, you know how moms can be. They pack lots of sweets, food items, instant meals, as if we're headed for a desert. I'm not sure if it'll feed the entire campus, but we can definitely throw a few parties with all this stuff."

"That's cool, dude. By the way, I just found out that we're going to be in the same department. We might even end up in the same grad housing complex. Your hometown buddy, Rahul, is graduating from the same department and moving on. I bumped into him a few days ago, and we got to talking about the department and campus life," Robi shared.

"That's great, Robi. I'm glad Rahul connected with you to help me out. It's nice to know we'll be classmates," Abhi replied, feeling a sense of camaraderie.

"Yeah, it's cool, Abhi. Let's start jamming, man!" Robi exclaimed.

Once they settled into the car, Robi turned on the music and offered Abhi a can of Red Bull, which he gladly accepted to refresh himself after the long journey.

"Gosh, this Red Bull is just the beginning, man. We've got more partying ahead, dude," Robi said with a mischievous smile.

Abhi noticed that Robi had a refined accent and was fluent in his communication. He instantly admired Robi's easygoing nature and saw the bond between them growing, despite coming from different parts of the world.

Robi's cool and exuberant behavior was captivating to watch. He seemed non-judgmental and carried himself with class. Abhi couldn't help but speculate that Robi came from an affluent family, given his outlook on life.

Abhi also observed that Robi was very tall, with sharp and athletic features. His height and demeanor hinted at his experience as a varsity basketball player. Robi mentioned that he had played NCAA basketball for two years at his previous college in Southern California, although he never pursued it as a career.

Robi rarely talked about himself, focusing instead on making Abhi feel at home and getting to know him better. Abhi found it heartening that they would be in the same department, albeit specializing in different areas. Abhi had chosen the general Engineering Economics program, while Robi had opted for Operations Research.

The two graduate students now found themselves speeding down South Bay Highway 101 towards the prestigious and verdant University Avenue in Palo Alto, the gateway to the Stanford campus. During the drive, they chatted away, relishing the conversation about their respective friends, families, parties, and even friendly dalliances.

Abhi was pleasantly surprised to discover the similarities between their families. Robi, like Abhi, grew up as a single child, raised by accomplished parents. Robi's father was a doctor, and his mother worked as a government officer in Los Angeles. They owned a mansion-style home in Southern California and spared no expense when it came to their only child.

Despite his privileged upbringing, Robi remained down-to-earth. He received more than he needed from his parents, from themed birthday parties to expensive toys and exotic vacations. He attended a private school in the same area, where he developed his basketball skills alongside a solid academic foundation.

Robi, on the other hand, discovered that Abhi had a similar charmed life growing up in India, hailing from a wealthy business family that placed great emphasis on education. The bond between them grew stronger as they realized their shared experiences.

As the Toyota Camry entered the revered grounds of Stanford University, Abhi's energy levels began to wane due to the jet lag. He hadn't gotten much sleep on the flight, with Robi's engaging personality keeping him wide awake. However, Abhi found solace in the fact that he was finally stepping foot onto the campus of his dreams and forging a strong friendship with Robi.

It was indeed a dream start to his Stanford journey.

Chapter 4

The Chillout Chronicles

The sprawling Stanford campus with its well-manicured lawns, neatly lined palm trees, and Spanish-style buildings spread over several hectares of land donated by the family of industrialist Leland Stanford, truly lived up to its reputation as a world-class institution. For many, gaining admission to Stanford meant securing the ultimate ticket to a world of opportunities. And for Abhi and Robi, it was a realization that was slowly sinking in.

True to their word, Abhi was assigned a room in one of the graduate housing halls on campus, just a few rooms away from where Robi had settled a few days earlier. Robi helped Abhi get settled in before bidding him good-bye. Abhi knew he needed to arrange his room and gather some basic necessities, but at that moment, he was more focused on getting some much-needed rest.

Overwhelmed by both homesickness and jet lag, Abhi made a conscious decision to stay composed and immerse himself in campus life and academics. He barely had the chance to unpack his bags and organize his belongings before exhaustion took over. After quickly freshening up, he collapsed onto his bed, falling into a deep sleep.

The following day was pleasant and warm in Palo Alto. The sun was shining brightly, and the clear skies welcomed the beginning of a beautiful Sunday. The campus buzzed with activity as students explored their new surroundings, jogging, biking, and finding their bearings.

Robi sensed that Abhi was still adjusting to the new environment and the effects of jet lag. Determined to help Abhi relax and settle in, Robi decided to introduce him to campus life in a more laid-back manner.

Abhi was jolted awake by gentle knocks on his door. Opening it, he found Robi standing there with a big smile.

"Dude, what's up? It's 11 in the morning! This isn't a refugee camp, man! We're in the Bay Area. Let's go out and enjoy the amazing weather," Robi exclaimed.

"Sure, Robi! I passed out as soon as I got here. It's hard to believe, but I feel completely out of touch," Abhi replied, still groggy from sleep.

"Alright! How about we have brunch? I know a great place on University Avenue where we can get some awesome food. Let's go, man. Get ready, and I'll be back in 15 minutes," Robi suggested.

Robi and Abhi embarked on their first jaunt together around noon on that sunny day, with a gentle Mediterranean breeze enhancing the atmosphere. Abhi was still trying to shake off the remnants of jet lag, but he was already feeling a bit better. They strolled into a trendy and prosperous downtown area, surrounded by fine cuisine restaurants, pubs, high-end stores, coffee cafes, bike shops, and extravagant office buildings housing lawyers and venture capitalists.

After relishing a delicious all-American breakfast, complete with juice and coffee, the two Stanford students wandered along University Avenue, keeping an eye out for good deals on clothes and other essentials. Abhi made an effort to stay engaged and combat his jet lag, while Robi seemed to be in his element, captivated by the sight of the young women—many of them their fellow college mates—who walked past them. His playful comments about the females they encountered were entertaining to Abhi. He noticed that Robi had a charismatic and classy flair, and though he had some casual dating experiences, he wasn't interested in pursuing a serious relationship. Robi considered it a distraction and preferred to have women on his own terms.

The abundance of women from over many countries at Stanford was not lost on Robi. He couldn't resist teasing Abhi, pointing out attractive girls in jeans and Stanford T-shirts, while also inquiring about his love life in India.

Blushing, Abhi replied, "Well, Robi, no girlfriends yet. I think there's plenty of time for that. Let me settle down first." He didn't want to reveal that, like many Indian students who had recently arrived, he was still inexperienced when it came to relationships.

"Wow, Abhi. At least you're not shy and nerdy! Alright, let's plan some parties and have a good time, bro! This is America—the land of opportunities and everything you could ever want! Can't you see? Aren't you going crazy, dude? Look at her, and there's another one—pure blonde," Robi exclaimed, gesturing toward attractive women passing by.

"No Indian girls for you, Abhi. You have plenty of them back home, anyway," Robi added with a mischievous grin.

Abhi smiled, quietly watching Robi's endearing nature. He wanted to join in the fun but decided to fully settle in and understand his surroundings before jumping into the social scene. Like any other "Fresh Off the Boat" (FOB) Indian student, he also wanted to be mindful of the money his parents had provided for essential expenses.

The dynamic duo, one dashing American and one gratified Indian FOB, headed back to campus to attend to their responsibilities and prepare for registration and classes.

Chapter 5

Beyond the Lecture Halls

Abhi had just a few days left before the first quarter classes began. He carefully planned out the essential tasks he needed to accomplish, such as opening a bank account, completing registration and fee payments, obtaining a student ID card and email address, shopping for necessary items and books, and taking care of other mundane matters. Additionally, he made arrangements to meet new people on campus, and he was particularly excited to attend some events with his friend Robi, as they always enjoyed each other's company.

Finally, Abhi found some time to set up his room, which turned out to be more spacious than the typical undergraduate dorm rooms. For now, he decided to rely on the dorm food and dine out at ethnic restaurants whenever necessary. Fortunately, food was not a concern at Stanford as the dorm meals, although bland, were manageable. On-campus restaurants and the packaged foods sent by his mom provided some much-needed variety.

Once Abhi acquired a local SIM card for his Blackberry, he could make and receive calls from home. However, he discovered that Skype was the preferred medium for staying connected, and regular calls helped alleviate his homesickness. He was pleasantly surprised by the significant number of Indian students on campus and the active involvement of the Stanford India Student Association in organizing various events. While there were plenty of Indian undergraduate students compared to

26

graduate and research students, there was also a notable presence of Indian faculty members. Abhi noticed that Indian guys were generally friendlier than the girls, although the Indian girls defied stereotypes and took pride in mingling with the general student crowd, even venturing into frat houses.

Abhi had no urgency to make numerous friends right away, but he recognized the importance of networking. He decided to adopt a methodical approach and immerse himself in the circles that Robi had already established in a short time. Robi's flamboyant and friendly nature, coupled with his gift of the gab, fascinated Abhi. He admired Robi's relaxed attitude and non-judgmental approach.

As the fall quarter began, the Stanford campus buzzed with activity. Living on campus allowed Abhi to experience the vibrant energy and dynamic atmosphere firsthand. Witnessing the campus come alive in just one week felt almost magical. The tremendous fan following for the Stanford Cardinals sports teams left Abhi in awe. One of his first campus purchases was a red Cardinal T-shirt adorned with bold golden letters.

After attending department visits and meeting his advisor, Abhi finalized the courses he wanted to take and began the registration process. He and Robi only had one class in common. Abhi was astonished by how quickly he was expected to complete the registration and start attending classes. Fortunately, he encountered no obstacles in opening a bank account, obtaining his social security number, getting a mobile SIM card, purchasing a used bike from a store on University Avenue, and obtaining his student ID, course materials, and books. Robi even took him to a few places off-campus to help him with his social security card and bank account setup. Abhi appreciated Robi's assistance and cherished their time together.

Robi, too, spent time socializing and connecting with people from different parts of the world. He effortlessly established rapport with individuals on campus. He displayed nonchalance when it came to registration and preparing for classes, believing that academic life should involve less effort and more fun. His primary motivation for attending classes was to meet individuals from diverse backgrounds, regardless of gender and race.

On a sunny Saturday, Robi and Abhi decided to explore the city of San Francisco before the academic rigor intensified. Robi managed to convince two girls he had known from Southern California, who were now living in the Bay Area, to join them. Lin, a ravishingly beautiful Korean medical student, and Imelda, a vivacious Hispanic girl attending the local community college in the Foothills area, readily agreed to the outing. Robi's persuasive skills impressed Abhi, and he looked forward to a fantastic day.

Abhi was pleasantly surprised and excited when he saw the two attractive women getting into the Camry. Watching Robi effortlessly arrange such a fun-filled outing for both himself and Abhi was just amazing. It was a well-coordinated social gathering on a pleasant autumn Saturday. They purposely avoided the typical tourist spots and instead explored beaches and popular bars at night.

Abhi felt at ease in the company of the girls, as he was accustomed to socializing with co-ed classmates back home. He found himself drawn to both Lin and Imelda, but it was Lin who engaged him in lively conversations and asked intriguing questions. Imelda, on the other hand, focused her attention on Robi, playfully showering him with affection whenever the opportunity arose. Robi thoroughly relished the attention he received from the girls.

Despite the constant chilly breeze, hanging out at Stinson Beach was a delightful experience. The beach was surprisingly not crowded, and Abhi couldn't resist capturing the moment when Robi playfully carried Imelda into the water, causing her to scream in both excitement and surprise. Abhi knew he would take countless more photographs of their adventures. Imelda quietly savored the company and made sure Abhi felt comfortable in his new surroundings.

Inspired by Robi's antics, Abhi decided to boldly carry Imelda on his shoulders. Robi couldn't believe his eyes and burst into uncontrollable laughter, showering Abhi and Imelda with high fives.

Robi and the two friendly girls made Abhi feel completely at home, and most importantly, dispelled his homesickness. Abhi considered himself incredibly fortunate to have met Robi. He never imagined, even in his wildest dreams, that he would experience such an incredible time within just a few days.

After enjoying a delicious Chinese dinner in Chinatown, the foursome decided to explore the vibrant nightlife of San Francisco. Abhi noticed that the city's nightlife was refreshingly different, offering a liberal environment where trendy bars were absent, and traditional establishments welcomed couples of all kinds. After some dancing with the two lovely girls, the Stanford buddies bid farewell to them and headed back to campus. It was a memorable outing for Abhi!

After almost a week of fun and socializing on campus, Abhi prepared himself to begin classes. Robi remained his usual nonchalant self, effortlessly gliding through their shared class, while Abhi had to put in some effort to stay on track. Abhi felt overwhelmed by the caliber and exceptional brilliance of his classmates. He quickly realized that he needed to go beyond rote learning and apply critical thinking.

Abhi also discovered that Stanford's academic approach was distinct. Rather than causing undue mental stress, the university aimed to guide students through a variety of topics by incorporating real-life applications and contemporary projects. Both Abhi and Robi managed to navigate the first quarter without major issues. Campus life was fun, and everyone they encountered was courteous and helpful. Robi proved to be a valuable support system for Abhi, exchanging class notes and assisting with projects. They made it a point to attend numerous campus events, including the Cardinal NCAA tournaments held on campus.

Chapter 6

Sun, Sand, and Gratitude: Thanksgiving Break in LA

The third week of November brought a well-deserved break for the students to celebrate Thanksgiving holidays with their families. Robi, who was headed to his parents' place in Los Angeles, invited Abhi to join him for a few days. Intrigued by the offer to explore Hollywood and its glamorous surroundings, Abhi hesitated at first but ultimately accepted Robi's generous invitation. The prospect of meeting Robi's parents only added to his excitement.

Before leaving for LA, Abhi decided to connect with other Indian students on campus, many of whom were also newcomers like him. With a couple of days to spare, he made an effort to expand his social circle before embarking on the Thanksgiving trip with Robi. He discovered that there were quite a few party animals on campus, but Robi stood out among them.

After reveling in some partying with his new friends, it was time for Abhi to pack his bags and hit the road with Robi. The idea of embarking on a thrilling journey with someone he had known for only three months felt like a dream to Abhi. He expressed his gratitude to his lucky stars and kept his parents and close friends in India updated on the exciting turn of events in his life.

The two young men set off in Robi's powerful six-cylinder Toyota Camry, cruising down Highway 5—the preferred route from San Jose to Los Angeles—at speeds well beyond 80 MPH. They later decided to take a scenic detour along the Pacific Highway, which would lead them to Santa Monica, closer to Robi's parents' home.

As they drove along the picturesque Pacific Highway, they made a few stops for lunch and coffee. Abhi found himself captivated by the breathtaking beauty of the coastline and the lush vegetation that lined their route. The traffic was a bit heavy, as many others were also trying to reach their favorite destinations along the oceanfront. Abhi was impressed by the disciplined riders on the well-maintained highway, and he couldn't help but express his admiration for the excellent work done by the National Highways department.

As the sun began to set, the two friends rejoiced the scenic drive through the city, away from the oceanfront. Soon, they would reach the suburbs of Santa Monica, where Robi's parents resided in a magnificent Tudor home with beautifully landscaped gardens—an unmatched gem in the neighborhood.

Despite the cold weather in other parts of the US, Southern California greeted them with mild temperatures, making it an ideal destination for the next few days. With their light attire, the Stanford students felt comfortable and ready to be welcomed by Robi's parents, Dr. Malcolm Bascom and Maggie Bascom.

Abhi took a little time to adjust to the enthusiastic greetings and warm hugs from Robi's parents. It felt as though they had known him for years. In fact, they insisted that Abhi call them Doc and Maggie, doing away with the formal "Uncle" and "Aunty" titles typically used in India.

After some initial conversation at the entrance, Maggie escorted Abhi to the guest room while Robi settled into his own well-preserved room, always ready for his visits. Robi and his parents made sure Abhi felt at home and comfortable in the luxurious surroundings. Abhi was overwhelmed by the opulence and impeccable maintenance of the house—a unique experience incomparable to anything he had seen back in his hometown of Chennai.

The following day was dedicated to preparing for a sparkling Thanksgiving Luncheon hosted by the Bascoms at their home, with a few close friends in attendance. Maggie had gone above and beyond, preparing the traditional turkey roast along with a variety of breads, soups, salads, couscous, baked potatoes, cranberry sauce, and a delightful selection of desserts. They also had an assortment of wines, champagnes, and beers to complement the feast.

Abhi, the only non-American at the luncheon, was warmly embraced by everyone, and Robi encouraged him to sample various wines and indulge in the five-course traditional turkey feast. As Abhi let go of his inhibitions, he mingled with people from diverse backgrounds, relishing the company and also becoming the center of attention for a while.

Suddenly, everyone expressed a genuine curiosity about India—the exotic land Abhi hailed from—and his family back home. Abhi didn't sense any superficiality among the guests; rather, they displayed a natural desire to imbibe knowledge. Many of them were keen to learn about Indian food, clothing, arranged marriages, and the emphasis Indian parents placed on education and cultural events.

By the evening, Abhi was exhausted. However, Robi's party spirit was still alive, and he convinced Abhi to join him in exploring the local bars—an established Thanksgiving night tradition. The graduate students had their share of revelry at a couple of bars before finally calling it a night.

Completely drained, Abhi was grateful for the comfortable bed that allowed him to rest and recharge for the upcoming adventures. Robi had planned several exciting outings for the rest of the weekend, avoiding the typical tourist spots and opting for places like Beverly Hills, Rodeo Drive, and even the Hooters bar.

It was at the Hooters bar that Abhi witnessed the pleasures indulged by some people in the area. Having glamorous models serving drinks and dinner was a unique experience that fascinated him. From a distance, Robi observed Abhi's enthusiasm and couldn't help but relish his friend's delight in the superficial aspects of life..

Abhi recalled John Updike's famous words--

"America is a vast conspiracy to make you happy."

In that moment, he couldn't agree more, feeling grateful for the remarkable experiences he had encountered since arriving in the land of opportunities.

Chapter 7

Jingle Bells, Casino Swells

Abhi couldn't shake off the sublime memories he had from his time in Southern California along with Robi. He yearned to relive those moments again. However, it was time to get back to the grind at Stanford, finish academic commitments, and prepare for the Christmas holidays. Abhi and Robi had grown closer as friends, frequently seen together at various events on and off campus. Being in the same department was an added blessing.

"Looks like you had a blast on the trip, Abhi!" Robi said with a sheepish grin.

"Thank you, Robi! I owe you a lot, man!"

"No worries, dude. I had a great time too, thanks to you. It was a lot of fun, no kidding."

After a hectic winter session on campus, Abhi and Robi turned their attention to summer internships and planning for the Christmas holidays. Before embarking on another adventure, they signed up for the campus internship placement, knowing they would secure placements in the New Year.

This time, Abhi took the lead in planning the Christmas holidays. He suggested a trip to Las Vegas, and Robi readily agreed, mentioning that he would join Abhi in Vegas after visiting his parents in Southern California.

Las Vegas, known as the Sin City, was gearing up for its peak holiday season visitors. Months in advance, the city prepared to entice gamblers from all over the world with its opulent casinos and creative marketing tactics. While gambling was the primary attraction, Vegas also offered other materialistic pleasures such as entertainment shows, nightlife, and extravagant parties, earning its infamous reputation as Sin City.

Abhi was determined to experience Sin City for himself. He knew that the extravagant marketing strategies targeting high-net-worth individuals with gambling habits wouldn't lure him. His main intention was to try his luck at the blackjack tables and enjoy some time at the city's main attractions with his ever-merry American friend, Robi.

A day before Christmas, Abhi flew to Vegas and checked into a budget motel away from the strip. After freshening up, he called Robi.

"Hi, Robi! How are things in Santa Monica?"

"Going great, Abhi! Busy with Christmas stuff. I'll join you in Vegas the day after Christmas."

"That's on track then. Will see you soon," replied Abhi.

With a sense of excitement, Abhi headed to Caesars Palace Hotel and Casino to try his luck at the blackjack tables. He was captivated by the extravagant world of Vegas—the sounds of slot machines and the boisterous cheers from the tables added a unique charm to the atmosphere. Vegas surpassed Abhi's expectations, and he could feel the money flowing freely around him. The reality of the city's materialistic fabric overwhelmed him.

Abhi decided to start with the blackjack table, a game he was familiar with from playing on his computer. Applying his analytical mind and conservative principles, he joined a low-stakes table with fewer players to hone his gambling skills. The dealer casually tempted players to wager high stakes, but Abhi remained steadfast. He had a few lucky hands, including a winning streak, which turned his $100 wager into $300. The rush of adrenaline surged through his veins, but he resisted the temptation to continue and cashed out his extra chips, ensuring he had money left for other amusement with Robi.

After a modest buffet dinner at the casino, Abhi called it a day, eagerly anticipating Robi's arrival and the continuation of their adventures. The following day, Vegas was alive with the spirit of Christmas—slow in the morning but bustling in the evening, with the Vegas strip crowded with people from all over the world. Abhi soaked in the atmosphere, capturing countless moments with his mobile phone camera. He explored the magnificent shopping centers and bars housed within renowned casinos like MGM, Riviera, Sands, and Monte Carlo. There was never a dull moment, and his camera overflowed with breath taking snapshots.

Robi arrived the day after Christmas and joined Abhi at the motel. With the Toyota Camry at their disposal, they were ready to paint the town red. The Stanford students relished the drinks served by glamorous bartenders at a nearby casino bar, becoming a bit tipsy. Although unsure about gambling in their inebriated state, they had an urge to check out some bars.

After a relaxing time at the bar, the Stanford friends managed to catch an electrifying show at MGM Grand. It was a truly fascinating entertainment experience for Abhi.

The following day, they spent more time at the tables before deciding to drive back to Palo Alto, reminiscing about their unforgettable time in the Sin City of Vegas.

Chapter 8

New Year, New Beginnings

After their exciting times in Vegas, Abhi and Robi returned to Stanford to focus on their academics. Abhi still felt a bit of a hangover from all the fun they had, and the damp weather in the Bay Area didn't help him recover quickly. However, they were eager to secure summer internships and wasted no time in signing up for interviews at the campus placement center. Both Abhi and Robi were fortunate to receive interview opportunities, mostly conducted over the phone. It didn't take long for them to receive internship offers through the campus placement center. Robi secured an internship with Merrill Lynch Investment Banking in nearby San Francisco, while Abhi had to wait a bit longer before landing a position at a fast-growing e-commerce firm: Amazon, based in Seattle.

"Dude, that's a relief! We finally have something lined up," exclaimed Robi, his cool and nonchalant demeanor intact. Abhi, on the other hand, was more visibly excited. This was going to be his first paid gig, and at the top e-commerce company in Seattle, no less.

"I'm doubly excited, Robi! It's going to be amazing, man! I hope Seattle offers a refreshing change. You're lucky to stay in the Bay Area," responded Abhi.

With their summer internships secured, the Stanford friends decided to celebrate. They gathered with their campus friends at the Tresidder Union Center for pizza and drinks, coinciding with the start of the colorful spring season in the Bay Area. They reminisced about their exciting times, including their adventures in Santa Monica and Vegas, all while soaking in the lively atmosphere.

The spring quarter at Stanford progressed at a balanced pace, with Abhi and Robi maintaining a lifestyle that balanced partying with exam preparation. As expected, they easily navigated through their academic commitments. Their focus gradually shifted towards preparing for their internships, eager to gain practical experience and earn some real money.

Leaving the campus and their friends behind for the summer felt a bit strange for Abhi. He had grown accustomed to the campus lifestyle, playing tennis and basketball with Robi and their friends, and enthusiastically supporting the Cardinals' basketball team. The intensity of their partying had also increased compared to previous quarters, but now the friends had to take a break for the summer.

Back in India, Abhi's parents were relieved and proud of their son's academic achievements and adapting well to the new environment. Abhi made sure to call them and Gayatri every week, finding strength in sharing his experiences with his loved ones. They were thrilled to hear about his internship opportunity.

Abhi and Robi had to temporarily part ways for about three months. Abhi wasn't particularly thrilled about going to an unfamiliar place and wished he had secured an internship in the Bay Area. However, he was determined to learn more about the future of technology, starting with e-commerce.

As Labor Day weekend of 2007 approached, Stanford buzzed with excitement. The majority of students who had left campus for vacation returned, reveling in the knowledge and experiences the hallowed institution offered in a free and impartial manner.

The big news on campus was Apple's announcement of a highly innovative mobile phone with slick interfaces. The pre-launch hype surrounding what would soon be hailed as the most innovative device of the century—the smartphone—had Abhi eagerly wanting to get his hands on one. He had grown bored of his Blackberry.

Around the same time, the campus also buzzed with the rise of Barack Obama as the Democratic presidential nominee. His innovative campaign strategy, aimed at defeating his closest Democratic rival, Hillary Clinton, in the primaries, set the stage for a strong presidential race. The internet was abuzz with campaign rhetoric, intense discussions, and dedicated volunteers sharing campaign information.

Abhi couldn't help but compare Robi to Obama. He saw similarities in Robi's mannerisms, communication skills, and swagger, if not surpassing them. In fact, he posted a picture of Robi giving a thumbs up on Facebook, captioning it, "Our very own Obama."

As a Democrat, Robi felt pleased to be compared to Obama but preferred to stay away from the limelight. He focused on enjoying the little pleasures of life—parties, movies, and sports. Education had always been a favorite pastime for the intellectually gifted Robi.

Job offers poured in at prestigious universities like Stanford, especially for students pursuing Master's degrees in Business, Engineering, and Engineering Economics. Robi, being a US citizen, received four offers, while Abhi, with an F1 student visa and requiring potential sponsorship, managed to secure only one offer.

Robi burst into the Tressider Union cafeteria, where Abhi was sipping coffee and working on an important assignment. "Hey

Abhi, I got four offers, dude! I just can't believe this man! I think I'll go with Goldman Sachs!"

"Congratulations, Robi! You deserve it, man! I received one offer and feel lucky considering my visa status. It's Merrill Lynch, the same place you interned at last year, dude!" replied Abhi.

Robi's celebration mode kicked in. "Cool! Let's celebrate, dude! Forget about the assignment; it can wait."

The two Stanford buddies hopped into Robi's Camry and headed to a popular spot in San Francisco for happy hour drinks. Driving on the picturesque Highway 280, Abhi's spirits soared. "This feels great, man! I won't have to ask my parents for money anymore. It's a generous salary, dude! Thanks to Stanford, we're in an enviable position!"

"Abhi, you deserve it, man! And we'll be living in the city, dude! Wow, what a deal! Let's party, man."

The celebrations continued into the early hours of the morning. Abhi was quite intoxicated but managed to do some planning with Robi. They decided to find an apartment together near the Embarcadero area and prepare for their upcoming professional careers.

Back on campus, the soon-to-be graduates eagerly wrapped up their coursework, preparing to embark on their journeys into the real world.

Chapter 9

Tryst with Investment Banking

The Stanford students breathed a sigh of relief as they completed their final academic obligations. Abhi and Robi finished their last credits and assignments, feeling a sense of accomplishment as they prepared for their next milestone—the start of their professional careers.

"Hey Abhi, I can't believe we're done, man! It feels like the past couple of years flew by in an instant! Are you planning to visit your folks in India, dude?" asked Robi.

"Nah, I don't think so, Robi! Maybe my parents will come over for graduation. Let's see! Right now, I want to focus on preparing for city life, dude," replied Abhi.

"Alright, that sounds cool, man! How about we finalize our place in the city?"

With the bright sunshine illuminating the campus, Abhi and Robi went around, catching up with their classmates and friends. They organized parties, joined in the farewells at the fraternities, and basked in the exuberant atmosphere.

It was an elated feeling for Abhi—giving high fives to his graduate housing mates, classmates, and other familiar faces on campus.

As summer reached its peak in the Bay Area, the fresh Stanford graduates embarked on their journey into the prestigious corporate world. Abhi and Robi packed their belongings into the Camry and headed north to the bustling city of San Francisco.

Finding a suitable apartment wasn't too difficult for them, thanks to Craigslist. They secured a small pad close to the financial district, allowing them easy access to their workplaces. Moving in and settling down proved to be a logistical challenge, but they managed to navigate through it all. The cost of their new place was steep, but considering the market conditions, it was a reasonable deal. The rapid transition into the real world felt surreal to them, as they stepped into a new era of cut-throat competition in the finance industry.

The Fourth of July weekend became a memorable experience for Abhi and Robi. They indulged in three days of party hopping—inviting friends over for barbecues and beer, attending wine-tasting parties in Napa, and joining a glittering cruise party by the bay. The last day of the long weekend was spent shopping and getting ready for their new jobs.

With confidence and grace, Abhi walked into the Merrill Lynch San Francisco office. The receptionist directed him to a large conference hall where new hires were undergoing multiple orientation sessions. Abhi's supervisor, John Wells, head of Equity Research, welcomed him with a brisk handshake and showed him to his cubicle.

Robi, on the other hand, had a more relaxed approach to starting work. He joined Goldman Sachs a few days after Abhi and hoped for a brief honeymoon period, although he knew Goldman Sachs was notorious for long hours and hard work. Robi was assigned to the strategic investments department and went through orientation and a break-in period. His team leader was cheerful and intelligent, but also a demanding taskmaster in true Goldman Sachs style.

Amidst the busy orientation and break-in period, Abhi and Robi had little time for themselves. Abhi found himself traveling to New York for collaborative equities research work, while Robi was caught up in the system, working long hours and relying on pizza and soda for sustenance.

During the last weekend of the month, the best friends decided to take a well-deserved break and headed to Lake Tahoe and Reno for a relaxing getaway. With more money in their pockets, Abhi and Robi had a great time in Reno—jet skiing, going on boat trips, and even trying their luck at gambling.

Both Abhi and Robi made sure to stay in touch with their parents. Abhi's mother, in particular.

Abhi grew increasingly anxious about the situation at his company and the prevailing uncertainty due to the housing market recession. On the other hand, Robi seemed unaffected by the events and assured Abhi that he would leave the banking sector if things took a turn for the worse. The Stanford boys were certain that a crisis was looming and suspected that many cover-ups were taking place. Conversations during lunch breaks and happy hours revolved around this impending crisis.

As expected, in mid-September, the crisis hit hard with the stock market crash, followed by major upheavals at AIG and Lehman Brothers. Bankruptcies and mass layoffs occurred almost instantly. Merrill Lynch was severely affected and had to downsize its workforce. Unfortunately, as Abhi was on a work visa, he had no chance of surviving the onslaught and was among the scores of talented individuals shown the door.

Robi, witnessing the chaos and realizing the blunder made across various fronts, decided that there was no future in such an uncertain environment. Even Goldman Sachs was not spared, with many projects coming to an abrupt halt and multiple departments scrambling for cover. Abhi's termination, along with that of many of his colleagues, came as a major shock to Robi. He wanted to break free from the toxic and depressingly viral environment. The writing was clearly on the wall.

In October, Robi made the decision to quit and moved back to his parents' place in Los Angeles. Abhi, shocked and without hope of finding another job during the severe economic downturn, pondered over his options. Robi suggested that Abhi join him in Los Angeles to start a new career path there. While tempted initially, Abhi felt that the odds were stacked against him. He remained in regular contact with his parents, who urged him to stay composed and make a wise choice. It was not the end of the road for him, as being a Stanford graduate would surely open up many avenues.

Armed with a decent severance package from his former employer, Abhi made the decision to return home for at least a year until the dust settled. He was about to board the Singapore Airlines flight to Chennai, with layovers in Hong Kong and Singapore. Robi and almost all their Stanford friends were at San Francisco International Airport (SFO) to bid him farewell—an emotional moment for the warm, fun-loving, and brilliant guy they had come to know.

Robi, though quieter than usual, gathered himself to give Abhi a warm hug and said, "Will miss you, man! Take care, and I hope to see you soon."

Abhi was reminded of the emotional farewell he received in Chennai two years earlier. Overwhelmed, he broke down, tears streaming down his face, as he hugged each of his friends before proceeding to the security check.

Abhi sent a cheeky little text on his newly purchased iPhone to his mom:

"Your wish has come true, Amma! Will be home soon. Love to you and Appa!"

Part II: Chennai, India

Chapter 11

Coming Full Circle

Abhi, battling severe jet lag, moved around his familiar surroundings like a zombie. The comforting and delicious food served by his mom, along with the constant stream of visitors, provided some solace. However, the sudden lack of direction weighed heavily on him. His favorite cousin, Gayatri, kept him company and helped him navigate through the unexpected turn of events.

"Abhi, go and meet your friends. Start playing tennis. Engage in something new soon," Gayatri insisted. Abhi's mom echoed her words, ensuring that he had the space to decide his next steps.

Finally, Abhi made the decision to relax and spend time with his friends by going on a trip to Goa. Five days at the Club Mahindra resort felt like paradise. He connected with his close friends and sought their advice on how to make the most of his time in Chennai.

Abhi's friend Chinnu, with a local Toddy in one hand and a cigarette in the other, passionately shared his thoughts. "Machan Abhi, don't look for jobs, da! You'll only get frustrated. Instead, use your dad's network to enter the tech business. There's ample opportunity for e-commerce and fintech companies in India. Just go for it, da."

It was refreshing to hear the local language along with solid advice from his childhood friend, Chinnu. His other friends were equally supportive and added in a jovial tone, "We can provide you with the seed money for your new company, machan! Don't worry!"

Cheers filled the air. Abhi felt a surge of exhilaration, buoyed by the unwavering support of his good friends.

He strongly believed that everything happens for a reason. He had witnessed numerous successful ventures emerge from his dorm at Stanford. He drew inspiration from his experiences there and the lessons he learned from the competitive world of finance. A renewed sense of energy flowed through Abhi. He embraced the party scene at the beautiful Varca beach, indulging in water sports during the day and dancing every night.

It was time well-spent in Goa.

Chapter 12

Finding Zen in LA

Robi felt a sense of relief and joy upon returning to Los Angeles—there truly was no place like home! His parents ensured he had the space to plan his future and work at his own pace. Robi had become disillusioned by the economic downturn, the corrupt practices in the financial industry, and the greed that had tarnished it. Witnessing people leave their offices with just a cardboard box and a severance check was a heartbreaking sight. Such ruthlessness seemed to be a hallmark of the capitalist world.

"Dad, it's a bloodbath out there! I couldn't bear to watch my friends, especially Abhi, lose their jobs," Robi exclaimed.

"We understand, son! I've never seen or heard of anything like this before. Following your heart is the right course of action. Now, focus on the future, kiddo!" his dad replied.

To distract himself, Robi spent time practicing basketball on the practice court his parents had set up for him when he was growing up. The court had never been dismantled, and it remained his favorite pastime. His mom made sure his favorite foods were prepared and stocked in the fridge, while his dad ordered craft beer and fine wines for him to enjoy.

Robi was immensely grateful for the privileged life his parents had provided him. Their upbringing had steered him through his academic career without any major setbacks or temptations like drugs, drunk driving, or overspending.

His dad invited him to play golf at the local club. Having taken some golf lessons there, Robi was able to match his father's skills.

"Robi, you should travel a bit to have a change of scene and do some deep thinking! Working for someone else may not be your calling. Explore the world of possibilities, son!" his dad suggested.

Robi became emotional and hugged his dad, just like he used to when he was a child. "I won't let you down, Dad! Thank you for the timely advice. I need to contemplate my next steps."

Robi didn't send out his resume or reach out to recruiters, knowing that the Wall Street bloodbath hadn't ceased. In fact, it had worsened, and many of his friends had been affected by the ruthless and criminal mistakes of others. He was surprised that there were bailouts, but no CEOs were held accountable. Lehman Brothers declared bankruptcy, which proved to be one of the largest in the US. AIG filed for bankruptcy as well, but eventually got a bailout package from the government. Most brokerage firms resorted to massive layoffs and reported unprecedented losses.

Wall Street was under siege, and the global financial markets had collapsed. Recession loomed, and government intervention became necessary. On November 4th, Robi and his parents cast their votes for Obama, hoping he would become the first Black President of America and lead the nation through the severe economic crisis.

On November 5th, history was made when Barack Obama and his vice-presidential candidate, Joe Biden, swept the polls and formed the government in Washington, DC. In January the following year, Obama was sworn in as the first Black President of the United States.

Robi's parents shed tears of joy. Coming from modest backgrounds, they had lived the American Dream and now witnessed one of their own holding the most powerful office on the planet. The new president promptly implemented a relief package that included a bailout for key companies affected by the financial storm. Despite immense challenges, the US Congress passed an emergency bailout package.

Robi kept Abhi informed about all the developments in America through his new iPhone. They chatted frequently, but on the day of the Presidential Inauguration, Robi decided to call his dear friend and catch up.

"Congratulations, Robi! I'm thrilled to see Obama in the big seat, man! You must be ecstatic!" Abhi exclaimed from thousands of miles away.

"It's an amazing feeling, dude! The country needs a guy like him to turn things around. Things are pretty dire here. How is it back in India?" Robi asked.

Abhi responded instantly, "Well, not much better! The tremors are being felt here too. There haven't been many layoffs, but everything is slow!"

The friends exchanged information about their current activities and future plans. Robi mentioned his desire to travel a bit and then explore opportunities, while Abhi indicated that he might assist his dad with his business before embarking on his own ventures. Returning to America wasn't on his mind just yet.

Robi missed Abhi deeply. He was sincere, caring, and always wished the best for Robi. The memories they shared in Palo Alto, LA, Las Vegas, Santa Monica, Tahoe, Reno, and San Francisco were truly unforgettable. Even during their arguments over trivial matters, they remained on the same wavelength. Their bond was strong, and it motivated Robi to learn more about the people, culture, cuisine, and developments in India.

In Robi's opinion, the US had lost an invaluable asset: Abhishek Kumar!

Chapter 13

The Gift of Serendipity

During January 2009, Abhi dedicated a significant amount of time to soul-searching, aiming to find a direction for his life and career. He realized that the Indian corporate environment was not suitable for him, struggling to adapt to its archaic practices and work culture. Additionally, finding a role that aligned with his educational background proved challenging.

Taking the advice of his friends, Abhi made the decision to join his father's well-established auto components business. The company was thriving amidst the booming automobile industry in India, particularly in Chennai, known as the Detroit of the East. His father was overjoyed that Abhi chose to join the family business and encouraged him to ease into it at his own pace.

Abhi took this opportunity to gain hands-on training from the capable team nurtured by his father and late grandfather. He immersed himself in understanding the intricacies of the factory business, both internally and externally, while requesting a salary that matched his responsibilities. The proud father and son duo joined forces to propel the business forward.

Recognizing Abhi's occasional loneliness, especially after work, his parents sensed the need for him to form a deeper connection. It was time for Abhi to find the right person to share his life with. His mother cautiously approached him with the proposition of getting engaged, acknowledging his maturity, grounded nature, and sensitivity after his two-year stint abroad. Though relatively young, Abhi was ready for this next chapter.

The Kumar household became a hub of parties and impromptu visits in March. Malini and Kumar resumed hosting gatherings for their Rotary friends and other close acquaintances from their early days, and many of Abhi's friends.

During his parents wedding anniversary party held on their sprawling lawns, Abhi was totally captivated when a young and stunningly beautiful woman, accompanied by her well-groomed parents, entered their home. Abhi was immediately mesmerized by this breathtaking beauty, later described by his friends as an "Apsara" (celestial maiden). His heart raced as he welcomed them and discovered that they were good friends of his parents from the Rotary Club.

The girl introduced herself promptly, "Hi, I am Janani."

Abhi's face lit up with a radiant smile as he greeted, "Oh, hi! I'm Abhishek."

Janani responded with an enchanting smile that struck Abhi like lightning. He couldn't believe what was happening. Their interaction was spontaneous, and they shook hands, admiring each other's presence.

Abhi couldn't shake off the profound impact Janani had on him. After a few drinks and mingling with his old buddies, he eagerly sought out Janani's company again. She was with Gayatri, sipping juice. Gayatri, in a well-timed manner, grabbed Abhi's hand and said, "C'mon, Abhi. Do you know Janani? Join us for a few minutes. She also spent some time abroad like you."

Abhi seized the moment. Buoyed by the influence of single malt, he asked, "Oh, wow, were you in the States?"

"No, actually in London for a year. Just got back! Looks like you just got back from abroad as well?" Janani replied.

"Yes, I'm back from California," Abhi replied, his charm and humility shining through.

Abhi and Janani hit it off instantly. It was hard to believe that they had been talking for almost thirty minutes before being interrupted by Abhi's mom, who called them for dinner. Abhi, in a chivalrous mood, fetched dinner plates for Janani and himself and guided her through the buffet spread. Their conversation continued throughout dinner and dessert. Abhi wasted no time in sharing his experiences in the US, particularly the close friendship he had forged with a local African-American student at Stanford.

Finally, a party that could very well seal my fate, thought Abhi.

Abhi mustered the courage to inform his mom and Gayatri about his fondness for Janani and his desire to meet her again. His mom was overjoyed, and Gayatri celebrated with high fives.

"Guys, hold on! Let's not get ahead of ourselves. Let me see if she likes me first, and then maybe we can become friends," Abhi said with a sly smile.

"Oh yeah, we've heard that line before, bro! Alright, I'll invite her to the club. You better be there, showing off your tennis skills to my dear friend," replied Gayatri with a wink and cheeky smile.

Janani and Gayatri arrived at the club while Abhi was finishing his doubles game. All eyes turned toward these two attractive women who entered, including Abhi's. His doubles partner couldn't resist a playful comment, "Wow, love is in the air, right Abhi? Lucky fella!"

Abhi and Janani instantly bonded, thanks to Gayatri's facilitation. After a brief chat with the infatuated duo, Gayatri excused herself to catch up with other friends at the club.

Janani asked if she had interrupted his tennis game, remarking on his intense focus.

"Oh no, I was done when you guys came in. It was fun and intense, for sure. Anyway, it's great to see you again, and thanks for coming over, Janani," Abhi said sincerely.

Janani replied, "Well, you have to thank your dear cousin sister, Gai, for twisting my arm and convincing me to come along."

"Great! Gai is always there for me, Janani! By the way, I hope I didn't take you away from your busy schedule," Abhi said.

"Not busy at all. I've been helping my dad a bit these days and exploring opportunities in the healthcare space," Janani responded credibly.

This piqued Abhi's curiosity. "Are you planning to start a business in that field, Janani?"

"Kind of! But I have to do a fair amount of groundwork first, I suppose," Janani replied gracefully.

Janani then asked, "Well, Abhi, do you have plans to go back to the US, or do you intend to work with your dad here?"

"Actually, that's a timely question. At this point, I have no plans. Maybe I'll work with my dad for a while and see how things unfold. It's hard to plan too far ahead, Janani, but you never know where fate will lead me to," said Abhi.

"You're a Stanford grad! You can practically call the shots, right, Abhi?" she playfully teased.

Abhi replied, "Oh, come on. Stanford may open some doors, but I need to find something that keeps me passionate and happy," expressing his deeper desires.

With smiles on their faces and positive energy filling the room, their conversation lasted for over an hour. Abhi felt deeply connected to Janani and believed she was the right person for him. He didn't want to rush into anything but wanted to savor the romantic path unfolding before them.

Between his work at the factory and frequent dates with Janani, Abhi felt a sense of joy and contentment. The scorching summer heat of Chennai seemed inconsequential compared to the warmth of love and friendship blossoming within him for Janani. He later discovered that his mom had already spoken to Janani's mom.

It's no wonder people say that Indian moms are fantastic when it comes to "M&A" – Marriages & Arrangements.

On Tamil New Year's Day in April 2009, Abhi and Janani formalized their engagement in a private ceremony at the Taj Coromandel. The wedding date was set for an auspicious day in June of the same year. The boy who had returned from the US was finally hooked.

Abhi felt elated and was on cloud nine. He called Robi twice to share the news and discuss the wedding plans. He even sent him pictures of the engagement ceremony. Robi called back and ecstatically expressed his happiness in his own unique way.

"Yo dude, it's hard to believe, man! You're seriously smitten! I don't blame you. She's incredibly beautiful. How did you manage this, dude? Ho ho ho! I still can't believe it. You've fallen hard, bro!"

"Thank you, Robi! It happened so suddenly. I just liked her instantly! I've decided to get married this June, and you have to be here bro," Abhi said ecstatically.

"You know what, man? It is a crazy place, but I'll be there. I'll come, no matter what it takes! For you, I'll do anything, bro!" Robi replied.

"Wow, that's frickin' awesome, dude!" Abhi exclaimed, leaping in the air with joy.

Chapter 14

A Soul's Odyssey

It was springtime in Southern California, with the sun shining down on people with less intensity. Robi spent adequate time playing basketball, golf, and running on the beach. He met with a lot of his friends, but meeting them did not feel the same as before. For the first time in his life, Robi experienced a profound sense of missing something. He felt it was the right time to get away on a long trip and take his mind off the prevailing somber mood. He was glad that Abhi invited him over to India.

Robi checked around for tickets to India with a couple of travel agents recommended by Abhi. He settled on a nice deal from LA to Chennai, via Singapore Airlines, leaving around the 10th of June, well ahead of Abhi's wedding date, and provided the necessary information to process his tourist visa for India.

Robi was filled with frenzied excitement! It was hard to believe that he was going on an odyssey to an exotic place on the other side of the planet. For the first time in his life, he would be taking a very long transcontinental flight journey spanning two days.

Just before confirming his flight tickets, he told his parents, "Hey, Mom, Dad! Guess where I'm headed soon? I'll be gone for at least a few weeks."

"Wow! Are you serious, baby? Where to?" asked Robi's mother with a beaming smile.

"Of course, Mom! I am serious! Our man, Abhi, is getting married, and he wants me to be his best man. I'm going to India! Oh my God! I'm now taking a cue from you to go on an adventurous trip, Dad."

"Wow! That's amazing. Abhi is getting married already? That's kind of quick, honey," exclaimed Maggie.

"Great to hear, son. Go for it! You still have the American Express card, don't you? Go ahead! But do come back soon," said his Dad.

After receiving massive hugs from his parents, Robi embarked on the mission of preparing well for the long trip. He called Abhi almost every day to get the travel logistics under control.

As the travel date approached, Robi started experiencing some nervousness, or what some people call 'travel anxiety'. Going through the process of packing, getting the paperwork done, and doing last-minute shopping was tiring for Robi. Transitioning from being a one-bag local traveler to a multi-bag international traveler was a major shift for him. However, he was getting ready for the big trip and started calling his near and dear ones to say goodbye.

Robi could not believe that the day had finally come for him to embark on this adventurous trip. His parents were happy to see him off at LAX airport. The check-in formalities were unusually swift for Robi, and the efficient ground staff impressed him. The flight from LA to Singapore, with a brief stop at Hong Kong, was absolutely world-class. It offered cocktails, delectable food, entertainment, and a friendly crew. A bit of snoozing on the flight helped him regain his energy level. The flight was packed, but Robi felt comfortable throughout, and his fellow passengers were cordial, extremely well-behaved, and enjoying the luxuries of the flight.

The second leg of his journey was a different story altogether. He noticed that almost all his co-passengers were in a hurry to get in and occupy their seats. It was a relatively short flight from Singapore to Chennai. He observed that the majority of his co-passengers were Indians, and many of them spoke a different language that Robi felt he had to get used to. The atmosphere was more boisterous compared to the previous flight, and the food served was thoroughly Indian, with lots of spice and oil. The menu card referred to it as 'Chicken Biryani'. After relishing some chilled beer and Biryani, Robi dozed off.

Despite the noise and repeated announcements from the cockpit area in multiple languages, Robi couldn't wake up. After about twenty minutes, the lovely 747 Jumbo landed smoothly on the Chennai International Airport Tarmac. People rushed to retrieve their bags from the overhead storage and hurriedly disembarked, pushing past other passengers. The air hostesses made futile attempts to maintain order during the chaotic exit. Robi, indeed, had entered a different world, and it had been quite an eventful start.

Feeling groggy, Robi experienced a touch of what Abhi had referred to as jet lag when he received him at SFO airport two years ago. The Chennai airport, though not as modern as Singapore's, was functional and handled a large number of people. Robi felt culturally out of sync, realizing that he had entered a completely different world. He witnessed a mass of humanity clamoring to get out pronto.

After a long wait, Robi went through the immigration counter, where his passport and visa were checked. Once he retrieved his bags from the baggage area, he started looking for Abhi, following the signs to the exit door as instructed.

The moment Robi walked out of the big glass-paneled doors, he was hit with a wave of heat, humidity, and noise. In an instant, he spotted Abhi rushing towards him, greeting him with a massive hug. Robi handed his belongings to the family driver, Vetri, who accompanied Abhi. After exchanging warm greetings, Vetri headed off to prepare the car for their journey.

"You made it! Wow, it's so good to see you, man. You look great even after such a long flight!" exclaimed Abhi, filled with excitement. He fondly recollected the day when Robi received him at SFO airport back in August 2006.

"Oh man, this is a different world, Abhi! Glad I survived the trip. You warned me, but I wanted to experience the thrill, man! I'm happy to be here and ready to have one hell of a party, dude! I sure hope to get used to this sauna-like weather!" replied Robi.

"Well, you will, for sure, Robi! So, tell me about the trip first. We'll talk about the rest over some sumptuous Indian food. I have so much to tell you about what's been happening to me and Janani," Abhi eagerly responded.

The long drive in the family Innova car was filled with chatter in Americanized English and jargon that was completely alien to driver Vetri. Robi made an earnest effort to get to know Vetri despite the language barrier. In his broken English, Vetri managed to share a bit about himself, with Abhi providing further details about his longstanding association with the family. Robi was amazed by the mutual sense of loyalty and respect between Abhi and Vetri, with Abhi even referring to him as "Anna," which meant big brother.

Overwhelmed by the sea of people and the traffic congestion along the roads leading to Abhi's posh residential area in central Chennai, Robi realized that the city was not as big as Los Angeles but significantly denser and more chaotic. Car horns blared every few seconds, and two-wheelers and cars seemed to disregard traffic rules, resembling a crisscross dirt bike race.

"It's a different life here, Robi! Anyway, you're in for some good times and perhaps a life-changing experience, fella," Abhi said with a broad grin on his face.

"So be it, man! I'm ready," responded Robi.

The Innova pulled into the portico of a spacious and splendid-looking house that had been Abhi's home since birth. Abhi's parents came out to the entrance to greet Robi in a true Indian style. Abhi's father was the first to shake hands with Robi.

"Welcome to Chennai, Robi. I've heard great things about you. So glad you could make it," he said, giving Robi a gentlemanly hug. Abhi's mom took hold of both of Robi's hands and gently pulled him into the house.

"Hello, Robi! This is your home! Come in and make yourself very comfortable."

Robi expressed his gratitude with a traditional Namaste and embraced them once again. He thought Abhi's parents looked even more beautiful and graceful in person.

"I've heard a lot about you, Mrs. and Mr. Kumar. Abhi was constantly talking about you and his little cousin sister, Gayatri."

"Yes, Robi! Gayatri is very much a part of our family. She's busy with the wedding preparations, but you will be seeing her in all the upcoming functions," replied Kumar.

Robi was shown to the guest room, which resembled a suite with all the necessary amenities—a large king-size bed, a TV, an air-conditioner, a desk with a laptop monitor, and an attached bathroom with a geyser and a modern shower system. He was already overwhelmed by their hospitality. Vetri carefully arranged his bags near the wardrobe. Robi couldn't help but ask Vetri, "Hi, Brother, do you live nearby with your family? How are they? Can you please take these chocolates for them?" Vetri initially shook his head but later agreed, swayed by Robi's charismatic nod, and shook hands with him once again.

"Tell me, Sir... if you need anything, Sir! I will drive you, Sir. In our Innova! Bye, Sir!"

"Hey, Bro! Call me Robi, please!" said the charming and handsome American to Vetri.

"Okay. Okay, Brother, Robi!"

Robi was asked to take a refreshing shower and join them downstairs for a light meal before bedtime. The cool shower and air-conditioning helped him regain some energy. It all felt too good to be true. In just a couple of days, he had entered an entirely different world! This place had a distinct culture and hospitality that was out of this world. Poverty and inequality certainly existed, but people seemed to move forward with life in a rather positive manner.

The conversation around the dining table was informal and pleasant. Both Robi and Abhi were served delicious South Indian food in tandem—chicken curry, fish masala, rasam, spiced-up veggies with roti, rice, pickles, and chips. Robi had never seen such a spicy spread before.

"Wow, Mrs. Kumar, this is amazing! Is this normal or specially prepared for me?" Robi couldn't contain his excitement.

"Robi, this is just the beginning. You'll have to get ready for three big meals every day and many feasts during the wedding time," said Malini Kumar with great enthusiasm and typical Indian feminine charm.

Abhi then proceeded to update Robi on all the recent events in his life, especially the wonderful human being named Janani who had entered his life. He spoke non-stop until dinner was finished. Robi listened attentively and couldn't believe how quickly and confidently Abhi had made his decision. He was in awe and admiration of his friend and couldn't wait to meet his beautiful bride.

Robi was warming up to Abhi's family and surroundings. It was a princely lifestyle out here. After a restful night's sleep, Robi woke up refreshed and started to regain his usual energy. The weather was unusually hot and sultry, but it was tolerable in the pleasant home where he was staying.

As Robi descended the stairs, he noticed a multitude of people working in a disciplined manner all around the house—in the kitchen, the living room, the patio area, and the garden. It was a harmonious domestic setting, and watching Vetri wash the car was a delight!

While taking stock of the situation, Robi found Abhi and his parents waiting downstairs to have breakfast with their lanky guest.

"Good morning! Come on over, Robi. Did you sleep well? Ready for some coffee and breakfast?" Abhi's father asked with warmth and affection, while he and Abhi exchanged high fives, reminiscing about their good old days.

Robi could sense that Abhi's mom was eager to spoil him. True to his assumption, he was asked to sit at the dining table while serving coffee, followed by an array of dishes he had never seen before. Malini Kumar skillfully explained each dish as she served it.

"These are rice cakes called Idlis, and the brown ones are Vadai. We'll also serve you Dosa, a rice crepe, along with Sambar and various Chutneys."

"Oh my God! Am I going to be spoiled with these delicacies every day, Mrs. Kumar?" Robi asked, unable to contain his excitement.

"Yes, my dear! You have to immerse yourself in our culture and lifestyle. You deserve to be spoiled, Robi!" said Malini Kumar with a twinkle in her eyes.

Abhi chimed in, and asked if Robi was ready for sightseeing, shopping, and revelry in Chennai's bars.

Despite the sweltering Chennai heat and humidity, the Stanford friends explored the city, visiting places like Marina Beach, CityCenter Mall, and indulged in some spicy lunch and chilled beer at the club. Later in the evening, they headed to a popular pub located within one of the city's five-star hotels.

After some cocktails and appetizers at the pub, Robi felt completely drained and unable to walk. The jet lag had taken its toll. However, he hugged Abhi and expressed his gratitude for the way Abhi and his family had taken Indian hospitality to another level.

But something deeply impacted him.

"Is this the real India, Abhi? I'm already witnessing two extremes, dude," Robi felt empathy for the people in the lower strata of society.

"You'll see it for yourself, man! A lot needs to change here. Let's talk more later. For now, it's time for you to get some rest, buddy!" replied Abhi.

Robi bid farewell to the Kumars and promptly hit the sack, quickly succumbing to sleep.

Chapter 15

Forever Altered

"The big, fat Indian wedding," as Abhi described it to Robi, was only a few days away. Robi was taken to a couple of special shops to buy appropriate ethnic wear for the various functions he had been asked to attend, from the Mehendi Ceremony to Muhurtham, followed by an evening reception. The functions were all set at different venues and on different dates. Robi was excited about wearing the traditional ethnic dresses but insisted on wearing his fancy suit from Beverly Hills for the reception, as he had already spent a fortune on it. Abhi encouraged his friend to go ahead.

A couple of days before the wedding Muhurtham day, the bride's parents had organized the popular Mehendi ceremony at Janani's palatial home. Although it was mostly a girls-only function, Abhi's and Janani's parents wanted Robi to accompany Abhi and get to know the cultural and ceremonial aspects. The Mehendi event proved to be a major turning point in Robi's life.

The late afternoon ceremony did not lack any grandeur, although Abhi mentioned that it was one of those low-key ceremonial events. When Abhi and Robi walked past the gate into the main hall, they noticed a lot of well-dressed ladies sitting together and conversing in true Indian style. They observed a couple of women with special conical packets and a greenish-brown paste called "*henna*" painting the hands of the bride and the ladies in attendance. Within a few minutes, all the attention turned toward the two dapper-looking men. Janani's mother rushed to usher them inside to a special couch and started serving them mocktails and appetizers.

Robi was overwhelmed by the attention he was getting. Abhi's mother pulled Robi aside and introduced him to Janani, who had just had henna painted on her lovely, smooth, and shiny hands. They were unable to shake hands, as Janani's hands were still wet with the henna, but she was able to give a gentle hug, and thank him for coming all the way from the States.

Instantly, Janani called over a stunningly beautiful girl to her side and said, "Hi Gai, did you get a chance to meet Robi yet? Abhi's buddy from the States?"

Robi looked at Gayatri and became speechless. He was captivated and mesmerized by her divine beauty and charm. She was quite tall, slim, and fair-skinned, with remarkably sharp features that reminded him of one of those glamorous models in the gold jewelry ads displayed around town.

Gayatri was yet to get her henna done, so she held out her hand to Robi in a sweet manner and said, "Wow, nice to meet you, Robi, and welcome! Abhi keeps talking about you all the time. I hope you are enjoying your stay."

"Very much, Gayatri, nice to meet you too!" stuttered Robi, lacking his usual flair and flamboyance.

"Well, just call me Gai! That's how everyone calls me."

Abhi butted in, "Wow, glad you guys got a chance to meet before the big wedding day." He turned to Gayatri and asked if she could explain everything about the Mehendi ceremony to Robi and requested the camera guy to take a lot of pictures.

"Hi Gai, paint one of his hands with henna. Will you?" said Abhi. Everyone laughed, and Abhi's dad encouraged Robi to go for it.

Robi couldn't take his eyes off Gayatri. Her impeccable English and her explanation of the cultural aspects were both crisp and easy to understand. His heart pounded in his chest as she held his hand while one of the ladies gently applied the henna. He was awestruck, feeling a jolt of high-voltage energy from Gayatri's exquisite touch.

Despite being captivated by Gayatri, Robi also appreciated the gentle teasing from the women and men around him. He felt like he was being introduced to a whole new world of ethos. Robi was on cloud nine, getting digital snaps of the artistic henna painting on his hand to share with his parents and friends back home. It was the perfect start to the big, extravagant wedding for Robi. As he reveled in the delicious food served by the well-dressed catering staff, he bombarded Gayatri with questions, constantly seeking her attention.

Finally, Robi exclaimed, "You guys sure know how to celebrate, man!"

The following evening, Abhi's friends and a few cousins organized a surprise bachelor party at a mansion near Santhome Beach. The party wasn't as wild as those in the US but had all the elements to make it a memorable celebration of Abhi's bachelor days.

The day of the grand Muhurtham ceremony had arrived. It took place at an enchanting beachside resort about thirty-five miles from Abhi's home. Robi and Abhi, along with their families, stayed at the resort the previous day, relaxing and soaking in the soothing ocean breeze. After a round of cocktails and a light dinner at the beachside restaurant, they called it a night.

The bright sunshine welcomed the wedding entourage to the majestic ocean resort. Robi received a note with his morning coffee, instructing him to get ready for the ceremony. The dressing ritual for the Muhurtham ceremony was culturally unparalleled, and Robi embraced the novelty and exoticism of it all. Abhi looked stunning in his traditional South Indian marriage attire—a creamy white silk dhoti and a matching silk shirt adorned with a stole called angostram, around his shoulder.

"Wow, you look traditional and, of course, very handsome, dude!" exclaimed Robi. "But I wonder, how are you going to pee, man?" he chuckled, giving Abhi a high-five.

Abhi explained that Robi's attire, sherwani, was a traditional wedding dress popular in the north and believed it would be more comfortable for an American.

Abhi accompanied by a small music band and close friends and relatives, embarked on a formal horseback ride to the Muhurtham pandal area set up by the beach. It was a joyous sight watching him, being led in a small procession accompanied by a local band trumpeting away. Robi had never witnessed such grandeur before; this was a magnificent Indian wedding, and Abhi was undoubtedly the Prince Charming!

Abhi was seated on a beautifully decorated dias surrounded by the parents of both the bride and groom. Robi was asked to join them in the main pandal area. A Hindu priest performed several rituals, and Abhi recited mantras unfamiliar to Robi. The atmosphere was hot and sultry, but the delightful sea breeze provided relief. The pandal area was filled with well-dressed men, women, and children, all adorned in colorful traditional Indian attire and exquisite jewelry. Robi felt transported to a different world, soaking in the vibrant atmosphere and the warm goodwill from the 200-plus friends and relatives in attendance. The temporary pandal setup, with its circular canopy, exuded grandeur and elegance.

As Abhi completed the groom's rituals, a pleasant yet high-decibel drumbeat and the melodious sounds of traditional wind instruments welcomed the bride. She walked in wearing a traditional red saree adorned with fine gold jewelry. Robi turned to Abhi and exclaimed, "Wow, your bride looks like a Goddess, man! She's out of this world. And look at Gai! She is resplendent in her bewitching green saree and matching necklace. It feels like a heavenly entourage is approaching us."

Abhi smiled, thoroughly immersed in the moment, and Robi was equally enthralled. He felt that this wedding was taking place in paradise. The families had gone to great lengths to create a momentous occasion for their children to unite in matrimony.

Robi eagerly captured as many pictures as possible with his smartphone camera, determined not to miss a single moment. Unbeknownst to him, he ended up taking more pictures of Gayatri. He found himself increasingly drawn to her unparalleled beauty and grace. As Gayatri entered the pandal holding one hand of Janani, Robi high-fived her, realizing that the occasion was steeped in tradition and being meticulously documented by a professional videographer and a dedicated cameraman.

While Robi was absorbed in the Muhurtham ceremony with its unique customs, he couldn't help but steal glances at Gayatri, who was completely absorbed in the occasion. Abhi expertly followed the priest's instructions, holding Janani's beautiful hands as she beamed with joy. The couple looked stunning together, a perfect match. Robi couldn't help but feel a pang of disappointment that Gayatri was preoccupied with Janani and he couldn't learn more about the nuances of the ceremony from her.

The splendid finale was about to unfold. Tears of joy welled up in the eyes of the parents, and the priest made a regal announcement that the bride and groom were ready to tie the knot. As the priest recited mantras fluently and encouraged the musicians to provide the traditional *"Ketu Melam, Ketu Melam"* music, he handed Abhi a yellow-colored thread embedded with sacred jewelry called the "Thali." With grace and chivalry, Abhi turned towards Janani, smiling, and tied the Thali around her neck amidst the rhythmic backdrop of music. The crowd of 200-plus attendees showered rice grains and flower petals on the couple in celebration.

Cheering, hugging, and handshakes filled the pandal. Robi noticed that Abhi and Janani were virtually mobbed by their friends and relatives. It was a delight to watch the couple immerse themselves in such joyous moments.

Robi was immensely happy for Abhi and Janani, recognizing that they were two remarkable individuals meant to be together. He relished the candid comments from Abhi's friends, flowing freely in their exuberance. "Man, you're grounded now! You're hooked forever, buddy."

"You've really settled down, man," exclaimed another.

The cheering continued as the couple proceeded with the follow-on rituals. Robi couldn't help but notice Gayatri smiling and encouraging Abhi and Janani to keep their hands together. It was difficult for him to take his mind off her. He had never encountered such grace and beauty before. Gayatri's intelligence and friendly demeanor only added to her allure. Robi felt an inexplicable and positive attraction towards her, and he wondered if she felt the same during their interactions thus far.

After about an hour, Robi was directed to the luncheon area along with the newlyweds and Gayatri. He felt elated being around Gayatri, showering compliments about her lovely dress and tastefully selected jewelry. Throughout the luncheon, Robi's attention remained on Gayatri. Despite her busy schedule, attending to Janani and Abhi's needs, she managed to provide crisp answers to Robi's numerous questions about the rituals. Robi was completely bowled over by the grandeur and rich cultural aspects of the wedding. It was not just a mere party; it was an elaborate celebration. The parents of both the bride and groom ensured that the union of love and the coming together of two families were celebrated with great joy and splendor.

The most enchanting aspect of the entire event for Robi was the indescribable attraction he felt towards Gayatri. He was completely captivated by her beauty, grace, charm, intelligence, and above all, her warm disposition. She was an unbelievably remarkable package, and Robi found himself increasingly drawn to her. He wondered if Gayatri felt anything similar towards him during their friendly interactions.

The wedding reception, held the following day at one of the city's top marriage banquet halls, was an extraordinary experience for Robi. Abhi and Janani, dressed like fashion models in contemporary Indian style, stood together on a tastefully decorated stage. The atmosphere felt heavenly and surreal.

Robi, wearing an expensive suit he had acquired from Beverly Hills for the occasion, was absorbed in the moment. He stood on the main podium area alongside his family members and Gayatri, greeting the countless well-wishers who patiently lined up to bless the lovely couple.

Observing the long queue, Robi thought to himself, "The Kumars must have invited half of Chennai." Curious, he turned to Gayatri, who looked resplendent in her contemporary Indian fashion dress, and asked if it was true that half the city had attended.

Gayatri replied, "Not quite, but close. Yes, my uncle and aunt are very popular in Chennai and have a vast network of friends and well-wishers."

Robi made sure to spend ample time with Gayatri on the reception stage. At one point, he asked her, "Gai, I hope I'm not bothering you with all these questions. You are the only person I can turn to after Abhi."

Gayatri was genuinely touched by his words and reassured him, saying, "Not at all, Robi! I'm glad you're immersing yourself in the atmosphere. You're such an open-minded and cosmopolitan guy!"

Robi felt flattered and was determined to live up to that image. He sincerely wanted to interact more with Gayatri. There was something undeniably magical about her.

Carnatic music played live, enhancing the ambiance of the reception. Although Robi couldn't comprehend the lyrics, he found the music smooth, melodious, and appropriate for the occasion. The only boisterous moment occurred when a group of overly exuberant college friends of Abhi stormed the stage and performed a celebratory dance, encircling the couple. Robi delighted in watching the impromptu performance by the spirited group of young men and women. Overwhelmed with joy, Janani and Abhi embraced each one of them, returning to the routine of greeting more guests, including some powerful VIPs, as mentioned by Gayatri.

It was undoubtedly a joyous, and unforgettable wedding celebration.

Chapter 16

Building Bridges in Singara Chennai

The entire trip was well worth it for Robi. Above all, it felt like Gayatri had come down like a manna from heaven for him. He wanted to spend more time exploring Chennai and getting to know Gayatri better.

Robi soon realized that he was now in a conservative environment and needed to be careful with his behavior, especially in front of women and elders. However, he managed to gather the courage to interact more freely with Gayatri.

Gayatri sensed that Robi was being friendly and not trying to be a cheap flirt like some men she had encountered. She knew that Abhi would not befriend someone who was devious in any way. In fact, Robi seemed far from that—he appeared legitimate and classy! Gayatri admired Robi's interest and enthusiasm for the cultural aspects of India.

Robi observed that Abhi and Janani were busy with several follow-on rituals, including one he found interesting and completely inscrutable—the ceremony called *Shanti Muhurtham*.

On an auspicious night after the wedding reception, a priest, along with a few elders and close cousins of the couple, chanted mantras and blessed them to begin the process of holy copulation. Robi had the privilege of watching the solemn but lively ceremony from a distance. Abhi's room and bed were decorated with flowers, and a large plate filled with fruits and a jar of milk were placed nearby. Abhi appeared a little shy but fully engaged in the ceremony. Janani seemed nonchalant and smiled throughout, encouraged by her cousins.

After paying respects to the elders, the couple was pushed into the bed room amidst applause, cheers, and playful comments from some of the men. "Abhi, take it easy on Janani; but go for twins, bro," and other similar remarks in the local language filled the air. Once Abhi's door closed, everyone dispersed, marking the end of a remarkable series of events.

The following evening, Abhi and Janani took Robi to the club for cocktails and a casual meal. They informed Robi that they were leaving for their honeymoon the following day and wanted him to stay back and see more of Chennai.

"Wow! That's great, Abhi. You and Janani deserve to savor every moment. Once again, I'm so happy for you guys and grateful that I was here for this grand celebration," Robi exclaimed.

"We're thrilled to have you here with us, man! You're part of our family, dude. I'll be away for a couple of weeks, Robi. Honeymooning in Europe is a treat, and time will fly by. But you should stay a bit longer until we return. I've asked Vetri to drive you around, and Gayatri can suggest some sightseeing spots. Keep this phone with the Indian SIM card. It has all the important numbers. My parents also want you to stay and enjoy more of the city. Have a great time, dude!" Abhi said, giving Robi a high-five.

"That's super cool, Abhi! And thank you, Janani! Let me confirm my return trip after you guys come back. You have a fantastic trip. Oh, by the way, wake me up early. I want to accompany you guys to the airport," Robi replied.

"Alright, that's a deal. Gai will be coming to the airport with us as well. Let's have another drink and look forward to more fantastic celebrations, Robi."

After bidding the lovely couple goodnight, Robi retired to his bedroom in the same house and started texting and sending more pictures to his parents and friends. One of his friends from the Bay Area responded after seeing the picture of Gayatri and Robi having dinner together in the wedding reception area:

"Dude, you're having such a blast! Way to go, bro! By the way, who is the goddess sitting next to you? Lucky man!"

Robi's parents were thrilled to see all the pictures and videos. In fact, with Robi's permission, they were proudly showing them to their friends. They couldn't wait to visit such exotic places. His dad sent a text:

"Glad you're having such a good time, son. Please convey our blessings to Abhi and his lovely bride. We are so happy for them."

The next morning, he woke up early to accompany Abhi and Janani to the airport, and he was delighted to see Gayatri there. His excitement was hard to hide.

"Hi, Gai! Good morning," he greeted her with a high-five and an effervescent smile.

"Hi! Good morning Robi! Are you overwhelmed by the ceremonies? Stay back and see more of the city!"

"Oh, sure. In fact, I'm staying back to paint the town even redder," replied Robi with a cheeky grin.

The ride to Chennai International Airport was filled with laughter. Robi noticed that Gayatri was witty and had a great sense of humor. She never missed an opportunity to tease Abhi and mention how smitten he was with Janani. After bidding Abhi and Janani a cheerful farewell, Gayatri and Robi got back into the Innova.

"What a lovely couple! They are perfect for each other. I'm sure they'll have a fantastic time in Europe."

"Yeah, they truly deserve each other, don't they? I'm so happy for both of them!"

"Gai! How about we stop by a nice coffee shop on the way? I feel like having a strong black coffee. No pun intended..."

"Oh, Robi! Are you already missing home?" asked Gayatri with an endearing smile. "Well, let's swing by the Le Meridien Coffee shop. Vetri Anna, please stop by the Le Meridien," she requested in Tamil. Gayatri's grace and charm shone through even more when she spoke her mother tongue, although Robi didn't understand a word.

Robi was thoroughly impressed by the opulence of Le Meridien Hotel. The elegant lobby served a variety of coffee, including Robi's favorite double-shot espresso. They found a comfortable spot in the lounge area and ordered their drinks—a double espresso for Robi and a cappuccino for Gayatri.

Over coffee, Robi expressed his curiosity about Gayatri's parents and her interests in life. They had an engaging conversation and shared a lot of information. Robi was fascinated to learn that she was trained in a traditional Indian dance form called *Bharatha Natyam* and also played the piano. She was planning to complete her Master's in Commerce and perhaps pursue an MBA afterward.

"Do you have any plans to study abroad, Gai?"

"Well, I haven't really thought about it. Maybe you and Abhi can give me some pointers," laughed Gayatri. "You know, it's not easy for a single child, especially a girl, to make such decisions."

Gayatri was impressed by what Robi shared about his parents and his upbringing in Los Angeles. He remained humble when discussing his achievements as a basketball player and his education at Stanford. "Well, I played a bit of ball in high school and college, and somehow managed to get through with the support of my parents."

"Also, Gai, what a coincidence. The four of us—you, Abhi, Janani, and myself—are all single kids with no siblings. Maybe we can start our own club!" said Robi, followed by uproarious laughter and high fives.

Gayatri was delightful and vibrant company. Towards the end of their conversation, Gayatri made an interesting remark:

"Well, Robi, did you see that famous coffee chain ad when we got out of the airport? 'A lot happens over coffee.' In our case, you managed to extract a lot of information from me," said Gayatri with a bubbly smile.

"So, a lot of BS over coffee, Gai! Hahaha!" Robi responded in his own relaxed American style. He handed his credit card, asked for the check, and requested the waiter to include two boxes of Italian chocolates for takeout.

Robi gave one box to Gayatri. "This is for you and your parents, my dear lady, and the other one is for Mrs. and Mr. Kumar."

"Oh no! You don't have to do this, Robi." But upon seeing Robi's unwavering insistence, she said, "Well, this is too much, but so sweet of you! Thank you!"

During the drive back home, Robi opened up a little more.

"I'm actually starting to like this place, Gai! The people are amazing, and the food is to die for, even though the crowd, pollution, and noise can be deterrents. And despite it all, you seem to be handling it well, and Abhi truly loves his hometown."

"There's nothing quite like home, Robi. We all get used to it, don't we?"

Finally, before parting ways for the day, Robi mustered the courage to ask Gayatri, "Would it be okay if I bother you to show me some interesting places in Chennai? It would mean a lot to me and help me get a better sense of this place, at least until Abhi returns," he asked with a sly smile.

Gayatri was initially hesitant but decided to show him around as she could sense Robi's sincerity. "Oh... um, okay! I think we can work something out."

Robi was glad that Gayatri agreed to his request, although he sensed her innocence and carefully orchestrated approach, which he presumed was typical of girls in India.

Robi made sure to check with Abhi's parents if it was appropriate for him to go around with Vetri, and Gayatri. He didn't want to violate any protocol. Malini Kumar had no reservations whatsoever and insisted that Robi explore the city with them and have a great time.

Chapter 17

In the Ebb and Flow

Gayatri had prepared an itinerary to visit popular tourist spots in Chennai and its surroundings. The list included Mahabalipuram, Dakshin Chitra, Crocodile Park, Tiger Caves, Valluvar Kottam, Marina Beach, and a straight drive leading to historical sites like Parry's Corner, Ripon Building, and the Museum. They planned to end the day with some shopping at the Citi Center mall near home.

Gayatri informed Robi to get ready for the day trip to the "Mahabs area," as the locals called it. Since she had to attend college in the morning, they decided to go in the afternoon. She also relayed the message to Vetri so that they could use the family Innova car for the trip.

Robi was ecstatic about exploring more of Chennai and its surroundings. He expressed his gratitude to Mrs. Kumar for the delicious brunch and for allowing them to use the family car and Vetri as the driver, and Gayatri accompanying them.

"Sure, my dear! Have fun! You shouldn't get bored here without Abhi. Let Gai take his place for a few days," Mrs. Malini Kumar replied with genuine affection.

When the doorbell rang, Robi went to receive Gayatri, who was dressed in casual semi-western clothes and looked stunningly beautiful. He couldn't help but compliment her, saying, "Wow, you look different. I've never seen you in casual attire, but you are stunning nevertheless."

"Thank you. I have to be casual and comfortable. We'll be outdoors in hot and humid conditions. You're dressed appropriately too, in a casual t-shirt and shorts," Gayatri replied, giving Robi a high-five.

"Hi, we're setting out to Mahabs, a popular tourist attraction. On the way back, we can spend time at the traditional Dakshin Chitra and maybe check out the Crocodile Park," Gayatri said with enthusiasm.

"Sounds good to me, man! You're the boss today, and Bro Vetri is our beloved pilot," Robi replied, making Gayatri laugh softly. She then turned to Vetri and gave him clear instructions in Tamil, which Robi found cool and sexy.

During the drive to the tourist spot south of Chennai, Gayatri bombarded Robi with questions about life in the US—universities, malls, highways, culture, fast cars, friends, and his career goals.

"Wow, Robi! America sounds like a land of milk and honey! But some say it's rather intimidating—the size, the political ideologies, the massive university system, malls, corporations, McDonald's, and whatnot!"

"Yeah, it's fascinating and different. A lot of wealth and opportunities, Gai! But I feel like India is also heading in that direction," Robi replied.

"I'm sure you have a lot of girlfriends, right? You're a nice catch for many girls out there!" Gayatri teased with a coy smile and a gentle pat on his hand.

Robi was taken aback by the question. "Woah! I didn't see that coming, Gai. Well, I have a lot of friends, but no girlfriend as such. In other words, I'm not in a relationship. I'm not ready yet. But if I find the right person, I'm sure I'll make a move. I want a stable marriage like my parents'. By the way, Abhi and Janani are an inspiration to me now."

Gayatri smiled, feeling that Robi's response was sincere. He seemed to have a solid value system and an independent thought process, unlike the people she had encountered.

"Do you plan to get a job again or try your hand at business?" Gayatri asked curiously.

"Not sure, Gai! I'm going to think about it a lot and seek Abhi's advice and input. He seems to have gotten his shit together! Oops, sorry. That slang just slipped out. Excuse me," Robi replied, realizing he had used a slang term.

Vetri skillfully turned into a small lane from the Beach Road highway, signaling to Robi that they had reached the first spot. The area seemed somewhat familiar to Robi since a marriage function had been held in one of the beach resorts nearby.

"Okay, here we are. This is Mahabalipuram: The pride of Chennai. This place was ruled by the kingdom of Pallavas many centuries ago. They were advanced even back then, and many of these temples and monuments have been preserved for centuries," Gayatri explained.

Robi immersed himself in the vibrant atmosphere. It was a small ancient city along the beach, surrounded by rocks, thick sand, and abundant greenery. Robi took numerous pictures and strolled along the shore temple and the rock area on the beach with Gayatri.

While Robi ventured closer to the waves, Gayatri firmly held his hand and cautioned him to be careful as the tide could become intense. It was the first time Gayatri had affectionately touched him and showed concern. Although Gayatri didn't think much of it,

Robi got a bit carried away and playfully nudged her, saying, "No worries, Gai. I'll be careful. I'm in good hands anyway. You'll save me if I get pulled by the waves, right?"

Gayatri was flattered by the comment and replied, "Oh, sure," before gently pushing him into the waves.

After visiting Dakshin Chitra and the Crocodile Park, they headed back home. The conversation became more subdued as they grew tired from the journey. They discussed music, movies, club life, college life, the Indian economy, and the popular sport in India: cricket.

"Are you serious, Gai? Do they really play cricket for five days? The English have left you guys with some serious crap!" Robi exclaimed.

The next couple of days flew by quickly. Gayatri had limited time to show Robi other spots within the city. Robi couldn't help but feel that Gayatri had cast an inexplicable spell on him. She was not only beautiful but also well-rounded, talented, and possessed a strong value system. Despite her wealth, she never showed it and was actively involved in charitable activities.

As Gayatri took Robi around, he noticed a certain warmth and sincerity in her that he hadn't seen in any of the women he had been with before. Also, he found himself increasingly drawn to the local Chennai culture, thanks to Gayatri's influence. He even requested her help in selecting Indian attire for him.

Robi couldn't deny that he had developed a deep admiration and affection for Gayatri. It wasn't physical attraction per se, but a sense of awe and wonder. He wasn't sure if Gayatri felt the same way, but he was curious to know her thoughts about him, considering they were relative strangers.

In the car, a silence fell upon them for a few minutes. Robi was deep in contemplation, trying to find the right way to express his feelings to Gayatri, even if indirectly.

"Well, Gai, we've only known each other for a couple of weeks. Are you comfortable with me and taking me around?" Robi asked, his voice filled with anticipation.

Gayatri responded with a ravishing smile, "Are you going to eat me? Just kidding! I'm comfortable, Robi. Abhi's friends are my friends, and it's nice to hang around with you."

Robi found her response inscrutable, unsure if that was how women tended to feel in the beginning of a connection.

Meanwhile, Abhi and Janani returned to Chennai after their memorable and fulfilling trip. They had visited all the planned sightseeing spots and made sure they spent quality time together. During their honeymoon, Abhi got to know Janani even better and appreciated her balanced approach to life. They bonded both physically and mentally, with occasional arguments that only reinforced Abhi's belief that Janani would complement his ambitions and lifestyle.

Vetri, once again, chauffeured Abhi and Janani back home. The joyous couple walked into an affectionate group of people waiting near the main door. Both sets of parents warmly welcomed them and bombarded them with questions. Robi watched the scene with a smile and eventually walked over to embrace Abhi and Janani with a big hug.

"Missed you, man! But Gai, Mom, Dad, and Vetri took great care of me. So, how was your trip, Abhi and Janani?" Robi asked, eager to hear their stories.

"It was incredible, almost too good to be true. Janani had me under control the entire time!" Abhi exclaimed with a broad grin and a wink.

"Well, get used to it, Abhi! It's good for you, man!" Robi responded, causing everyone to burst into laughter.

After a delightful brunch with the whole family, Abhi and Robi decided to have some private time on the terrace. They promptly updated each other on everything that had happened in their lives during the past week or so.

Robi couldn't help but express his gratitude again, saying, "Your parents, Gai, and Vetri took such good care of me, man. I felt like a prince. There's some kind of magnetic pull I'm experiencing here in Chennai."

"You deserve it, Robi. I'm glad you had a wonderful time. It's all reciprocal. I'll never forget the hospitality your parents extended to me when I was in LA," Abhi replied sincerely.

"Oh, come on. Let's not keep score here. Your folks went above and beyond, surpassing all expectations. Seriously, I've never eaten so much food in my life or taken so many pictures and videos in such a short time," Robi said.

"Well, then, maybe you should write a book about it, Robi!" Abhi suggested, causing laughter to fill the air. The Stanford buddies were bonding once again. Abhi expressed his desire to spend more time with Robi, seeking his input on starting a new business.

"Stay for a couple more weeks, Robi! I need your insights for the business I want to pursue," Abhi proposed earnestly.

"That's incredibly sweet of you! I'm not sure, man. I also need to figure things out. Okay, let me stick around for a few days. I need your help in shaping my future as well," Robi replied.

"That's my man! We are both adventurous and risk takers. Let us embark on a real start up here man! We should talk more along those lines. So, keep your return ticket open for now. We'll decide once we've had some solid discussions and, of course, after partying some more!" Abhi exclaimed with excitement, exchanging high fives with Robi.

Chapter 18

Breaking into Uncharted Territory

Abhi decided to take Robi to his dad's factory to brainstorm about starting a new venture in Chennai. They were interested in a startup that would align with the Silicon Valley ecosystem, leveraging their network in the US for solid growth.

Robi was brought to a simple yet elegantly designed factory-cum-office building on the outskirts of the city. It was a fascinating experience for him to witness Abhi skillfully navigating through the congested roads filled with two-wheelers, three-wheelers, four-wheelers, and pedestrians. It was a different world for Robi, but Abhi seemed right at home.

After a quick tour of the factory, they settled down in Abhi's swanky office for a cup of coffee and a business discussion.

"Robi, I think it's the perfect time to start an internet technology company in India. We can explore options like niche e-commerce, high-end web design services, or even back-end transaction services for US-based e-commerce companies. We can establish the company here and expand operations to North America and other international regions," Abhi proposed.

"Interesting, Abhi! Let's first identify a solid growth opportunity and then work out the logistics of getting started.

We need to consider funding, office setup, operational launch, and everything else. With our complementary skills, we can find the sweet spot without overanalyzing," Robi responded.

After several rounds of brainstorming, the Stanford buddies decided to focus on developing a cutting-edge e-commerce site that specialized in selling electronic gadgets. Abhi's short stint as intern at Amazon helped a great deal to do the planning. They aimed to create a dynamic and innovative website that aggregated electronic devices from various branded manufacturers, providing intuitive graphics, user-friendly interfaces, and efficient transactional capabilities. They planned to develop a detailed business plan and conduct a competitive analysis of the Indian market.

Initially, Robi was hesitant to extend his stay, but the opportunity to start a business with Abhi and spend more time with Gayatri convinced him to take the plunge.

A couple of days later, while having beers at the club, Robi shook hands with Abhi and made a firm commitment, "Let's do it, man! I'm ready to give this startup a serious shot. I see great potential and opportunity. Let's become co-founders, pool in some money, and go for it."

"That sounds fantastic, Robi! I'm thrilled, dude! We can start by drawing up some preliminary papers, opening a bank account, and getting all the necessary groundwork done. We can even approach my dad for some seed money," Abhi exclaimed with enthusiasm.

"Sure, Abhi. We can ask our respective parents for some angel money. We need to get this off the ground, dude! Cheers to that. Life has taken an unexpected turn. Just a year ago, we were enjoying the luxurious investment banker lifestyle, and now we're going to be starving entrepreneurs," Robi remarked.

Abhi smiled and reflected on how things had changed, saying, "Hopefully for the better, Robi! You have real guts to dive into this foreign land. Kudos to you."

Abhi and Robi exchanged their customary high fives and knuckles before deciding to head home and get some rest, driven by their adventurous spirit.

Robi felt comfortable with the decision to enter the startup world, even though it was quite unusual to start something so new and far from home. He made calls to his parents to seek their consent and inquire about seed funding. Initially surprised, his parents believed that the two buddies had enough brain-power to figure things out. So, they committed their full support.

The next call Robi made was to Gayatri. "Hey, Gai! Guess what! A major turn of events here. Abhi and I have decided to start a company. I'm extending my stay a bit longer to get things off the ground. I'm thoroughly excited!"

"Wow! You guys are really going for it. Will I easily find a job in your company, Robi? Can you put in a good word for me?" Gayatri asked warmly.

"Well, would you consider joining our company, dear lady? You're super-smart and perhaps way too accomplished!" Robi imagined Gayatri blushing at the other end of the line.

"I'm not sure if you can afford me! Hehehe..." Gayatri replied playfully.

"Well, Gai, as you can imagine, Abhi and I are moving fast on this. I need to work out my stay logistics. I'll have to find a service apartment or something nearby. It wouldn't be fair to burden Abhi and his parents any further. Plus, I want to be independent here. I'll keep you posted, Gai. Good night, kiddo!" Robi explained.

"Don't worry, it will all work out. You Stanford guys are like manna from heaven. Good luck and good night, hotshot!" Gayatri teased before ending the call.

Robi was still trying to grasp the rapid pace of events. He constantly contemplated adapting to a completely different environment, including work culture, unknown market territory, cash-flow challenges, bureaucracy, and various operational obstacles. With Abhi by his side, he felt confident that they could overcome these challenges.

The following day, Robi asked Abhi to help him find a service apartment nearby so he could have his independence and avoid inconveniencing his parents.

"Are you sure, Robi? It's just a short time, and it's no trouble for my parents or me. You're not an extra burden; you're a fun family member to have around," Abhi expressed.

"That's really touching, my friend. But, no. Let's do this right, Abhi. I need to stand on my own feet and learn to survive, no matter how tough it gets. Please, don't have any hard feelings. Help me find a decent service apartment," Robi insisted.

Eventually, Abhi agreed, and with his parents' consent, he contacted one of his club friends to secure a service apartment in the same area. Abhi and his father also decided to take care of the visa formalities to ensure that Robi could stay for an extended period.

Chapter 19

Brave Beginnings

Robi and Abhi quickly realized that starting a company in India was akin to bringing a baby into the world, with the added challenge of navigating through a mountain of paperwork. Robi acquired the domain name 'Gadgets Online,' and the founders promptly decided to register both the domain name and the company under the same name.

The pace was relentless as they met with lawyers, accountants, bank representatives, ROC consultants, RBI officials and key contacts across various locations in the tropical heat. Abhi's father proved to be a valuable asset, facilitating the progress of the paperwork and arranging the necessary work visa for Robi to stay back.

Finally, Robi and Abhi settled into their new roles. Gayatri and Janani provided invaluable assistance in setting up the furniture, workstations, and a small pantry area for coffee and tea. Robi found it refreshing to have Gayatri in the office, observing her subtle instructions to the male staff members to establish an efficient office routine.

By mid-August, a web developer, Anoop, and a database programmer, Goks, had joined the team to get the site up and running. They aimed for a visually appealing front-end and a robust transactional back-end, adopting a lean and efficient approach to their e-commerce startup.

Abhi and Robi found their rhythm. Realizing that a formal structure was not yet feasible, they divided their focus areas and worked as a team. Robi delved into marketing, devising a rapid action plan to drive traffic to the site upon its launch. He reached out to his Stanford connections and considered seeking input from Gayatri, who was studying commerce and economics.

Leaning on his Amazon stint, Abhi was able to focus on establishing the gadget taxonomy, identifying key device manufacturers to be featured on the site, and handling workflow and fulfillment aspects. Together, they worked on securing supply agreements to ensure smooth transactions.

During a team meeting, Abhi urged everyone to expedite website development and the transaction engine. He encouraged the tech team to seek the assistance of consultants for polishing the graphical user interface (GUI) and initiating testing.

Robi chimed in, "I'll help with the dry runs. Also, feel free to share your ideas on attracting more visitors to our site. I'm getting input from a buddy at Stanford, but local insights would be valuable too."

"Sure, Sir!" responded the tech team members confidently.

"Hey, Anoop! Just call me Robi, man. Why so formal? Relax! The same goes for Abhi as well, right, Abhi?"

"Oh yes, Sir!" Abhi exclaimed, and they all burst into laughter.

Goks, the more audacious of the two, asked, "Can I call you dude?" and grinned playfully.

"Absolutely! I love it, man. Give me a high five, dude!" Robi encouraged. The young techies noticed that both Abhi and Robi

spends all the time and money at the club," Gayatri shared with a measured laugh.

"By the way, Abhi mentioned that you and he practically grew up together," Robi continued.

"Yes, definitely. We went to the same school, with a two-year age gap. We spent most weekends together and frequented the club. He has always been a caring brother and protective of me. I don't feel like I'm missing out on having a sibling because Abhi is always there for me," Gayatri expressed warmly.

"Wow, that's wonderful to hear. He talks about you all the time. He's an amazing guy. I'm lucky to have him as a friend," Robi praised.

"Hey, you never told me much about your parents. Are they as tall and smart as you?" Gayatri inquired, turning the conversation around.

"They are quite tall, typical African American stock. I'd like to think they're smart too. My dad is a doctor, a surgeon at a large hospital in LA, and my mom works in the administration department for LA County. They've done well, Gai. More importantly, they invested a lot in raising me. They are very cool, and they take part in a lot of social activities and sports," Robi explained.

"What an impressive background! I hope to meet them someday. And why don't you have any siblings? If you don't mind me asking," Gayatri questioned.

"I suppose nature didn't bless my parents with another child. We wanted to adopt, but their careers didn't allow it. Life goes on, I guess," Robi reflected.

"And here you are in Chennai, talking to a lovely lassie. Quite the turn of events!" Gayatri teased.

"Well, you're more than a lovely lassie! If I may say so, you're incredibly beautiful, smart, and caring," Robi complimented.

Gayatri blushed, momentarily speechless. She smiled in response. "You're very kind, Robi."

"Oh, and thanks again for the delicious food. Can you cook as well as your mom?" Robi asked, raising his hand for a high-five and giving a gentle nudge.

"Well, I try..." Gayatri replied, returning the high-five.

"I better let you go, Gai. Is Vetri waiting?" Robi inquired.

"Yes, he is. Let me get going, Robi. Adios, amigo!" Gayatri bid farewell.

"Wow, that's cool. Come over again sometime, Gai!" Robi walked her to the entrance and unintentionally planted a gentle kiss on her cheek.

Moved by the gesture, Gayatri gave him a gentle hug before sauntering out.

Robi felt like he was on a different planet that night. He hadn't expected his life to take such a dramatic turn in a matter of weeks.

Robi had developed a strong fondness for Gayatri and made sure to express his feelings whenever possible. The intensity of his emotions puzzled even him. It wasn't a simple physical attraction but a deep intellectual connection and affection towards someone he found to be extraordinary in many ways.

However, Robi remained unsure about Gayatri's feelings regarding their interactions and conversations. She had mentioned once that she was focused on friendship and appreciated the sincere affection. She reciprocated and was responsive, never creating any barriers or playing hard to get. She simply conveyed her state of mind at that point in time.

Robi reluctantly acknowledged that it could be challenging for a foreigner to integrate into mainstream Indian society, despite being captivated by its culture and the warmth of its people. Abhi had generously guided him through the nuances, but it was Gayatri who wholeheartedly introduced him to the entire cultural scene. Both Abhi and Gayatri made him feel like he belonged, erasing any sense of being a foreigner.

Working alongside Abhi, Anoop, and Goks was an absolute delight for Robi. It was stimulating and joyful to collaborate with all of them. The work environment was humbler than what he had experienced in the US, but these young engineering talents had a nerdy streak while possessing a broader knowledge of the world. Robi effortlessly blended into the work environment.

Anoop and Goks had a good command of English, albeit with a slight accent. Gokul, affectionately called "Goks" by everyone hailed from a small town in the southern part of the state. He had studied Engineering in Chennai and worked at a mid-size IT services firm for two years before joining Gadgets Online. Anoop, on the other hand, grew up in Kerala, the neighboring state, and was multilingual. He pursued a degree in Computer Science and joined the startup after a brief stint at a firm in Bangalore, where he eventually connected with Abhi for a better job opportunity.

The mornings at "Gadgets Online" started off energetically with a hot cup of filter coffee served by a catering contractor. Robi settled into his small, open cubicle with his coffee in hand.

"Hey Goks, how was the weekend, man? Any girlfriends yet?" Robi asked with a mischievous grin.

"It was good, Robi. Oh, it's hard to find girlfriends in Chennai, dude," Goks replied with a coy smile.

"Really, Goks! You're a charming dude! You shouldn't have any problems!" Robi teased.

"Maybe in America, Robi. It seems easier there. I'm sure you have lots of girlfriends there," Goks responded, surprising Robi.

"Wow, Goks, you've got an American fetish too! Why not? Let's work on it, dude?" Robi suggested with a high-five.

Anoop joined the conversation and added, "Count me in, Robi!"

"Wow, Anoop, my man! You're interested too!" exclaimed Robi, giving a big thumbs up to both of them. "Love you guys!"

"Sounds good, dude," the young techies replied in unison.

"Alright, let's get ready for our team meeting. Abhi should be here any minute."

Robi and the young turks got to work, clicking away on their computers. Robi worked on signing up as many partners as possible.

The team meeting that followed was casual and focused on keeping things on track. Robi knew that Abhi had a flair for operational details, so he allowed him to handle the internal day-to-day tasks without unnecessary interference. Robi, meanwhile, focused on the external aspects of marketing, business development, and partnerships.

Once the action items were discussed in the meeting, the team dispersed, exchanging high fives as they went about their tasks.

Chapter 20

In the Zone

Janani and Gayatri made regular visits to the office, bringing food, local snacks, and juice packets while interacting with everyone. The boys' faces lit up with big smiles whenever the ladies were around. Robi noticed that Gayatri effortlessly conversed with the young talents, switching between English and the local language.

Dressed in a traditional yet classy college attire—a kurti and jeans—Gayatri caught the attention of the young techies as she walked towards them.

"Hi, Goks and Anoop! *Eppadi Pothu?*" Gayatri greeted them in colloquial Tamil, leaving Robi scrambling for a translation, while Abhi chuckled silently in his cubicle.

"*Nalla Pothu,* Gayatri. Thank you. How are you? Thanks for all the food. Super *Sappadu!*" Goks replied, with Anoop nodding in agreement.

"*Seri, seri*! Hope these two Stanford boys are treating you guys okay," she winked at them with a stylish grin.

Robi interjected, "Hi, Gai! They are taking care of us, man! They are going to come up with world-class stuff soon."

"Anyways, are you done with college today? How about joining us for lunch? We can go to some nearby restaurant," Robi suggested.

"Oh, is it a company lunch or casual lunch?" Gayatri inquired.

Abhi seized the opportunity to join in, saying, "Already planned out, guys? Let us go to Benjarong Thai restaurant guys. It is a casual lunch on the company's dime. Gai, join us, please?"

"Okay, bro. Love hanging out with you guys!" Gayatri eagerly agreed, wearing an enthusiastic smile.

High fives were exchanged all around.

"Maybe we should change the company name to High Fives," Abhi chuckled.

The lunch outing at the Benjarong Thai restaurant was a total blast. The entire team, including Gayatri, indulged in a fabulous three-course authentic Thai meal.

"Oh, this place is fancy! Thai food in Chennai? I didn't expect this, dude!" Robi exclaimed.

During lunch, Robi got a chance to socialize with Gayatri even better. He asked her to translate the local slang so he could catch up with the local lingo. Gayatri made gentle fun of Robi and the young talents whenever she got the chance.

"Gai, why don't you become a team member at our little startup? The maestros here can teach you a lot of stuff. Won't you, guys?" Robi suggested with a wide smile.

"Oh, of course, sure! Anything for Gai!" Goks enthusiastically replied.

"Well, she has to finish her coursework, guys," Abhi interjected. "But Gai, you can come anytime and maybe do a small project as part of your coursework."

"Okay, okay. That's generous, Abhi. Let's see. I have no problem hanging out with you guys whenever I have time. Maybe I can help out with the office admin stuff for now," Gayatri offered.

"Oh, great. Let's get moving, guys. That was some fabulous lunch!" Robi declared.

September proved to be a busy month for the startup team at Gadgets Online. Gayatri and Janani assisted with administrative tasks and provided creative inputs. They made sporadic trips to the workplace, and the team was always eager to see them.

With the help of Janani and Gayatri, Abhi and Robi designed a company logo. During the logo design process, they stumbled upon a shorter and catchier name. They decided to brand their website as GOLI, an acronym for Gadgets Online.

"I think it's extra cool, easy to pronounce, and remember," Gayatri was the first to approve of the brand name GOLI, as it also meant "marble toys" in Tamil, giving it a great zing.

Everyone else quickly fell in line. Robi gave Gayatri a gentle hug and said, "Wow, you killed it, Gai! Gai's GOLI! It's all coming together, man."

Gayatri blushed, basking in the praise showered upon her. As they left the office, she invited Robi, Abhi, and Janani to join her for a casual chat at a popular coffee joint called Amethyst, along with some of her friends. Abhi and Janani declined due to prior commitments, but Robi agreed since he didn't have much to do anyway.

Following Gayatri's instructions, Robi took an autorickshaw to the supposedly sought after coffee joint. He was thoroughly impressed by the elegant setting of Amethyst, housed in a large mansion. The place was tastefully designed and decorated, offering both indoor and outdoor seating. It attracted wealthy locals, non-resident Indians, and expats like Robi. It had a cosmopolitan atmosphere, idyllic garden setting, book store and a coffee bar cum restaurant serving a mix of continental and exquisite local food.

Gayatri approached Robi, who seemed awestruck by the place, and guided him to a table where three of her friends—Anushya, Nikitha, and Shruti—were already seated. They introduced themselves and shook hands with Robi in an elegant manner that left him impressed.

"Nice to meet you all, and I hope I'm not intruding... Actually, I'm so glad Gai invited me. This place is just amazing. Wow, I'm so impressed!" Robi expressed his admiration.

"Glad you could join us, Robi," Anushya, a med student, replied. "Heard that you and Abhi were together at Stanford."

"Yeah, yeah! We had a great time together, and he was my closest buddy at Stanford. Glad he got me over to Chennai. This place has the best bars, coffee shops, sports clubs, malls, exotic restaurants, and lip-smacking food. I'm having the time of my life!" Robi exclaimed.

Nikitha and Shruti mentioned that they had spotted Robi at Abhi's wedding reception but hadn't had the chance to meet him. "Well, we were both wondering who the tall, handsome guy who looked like a basketball player was."

"Ladies! You've made my day. I never thought of myself like that. I'm just a happy-go-lucky guy working on the business we've started here, and, of course, savoring Chennai's hospitality. It's just out of the world!" Robi responded with a touch of humility.

"Well, I don't know how I missed you, lovely ladies, at the wedding. My bad," Robi admitted with a polished grin.

"Maybe there were too many good ones for you to choose from, Robi," Shruti teased.

"Well, you got me there!" Robi conceded.

The conversation shifted from life in the United States to Robi's family and friends in Los Angeles, as they relished the gourmet food on offer.

Robi candidly shared his experiences in Chennai, saying, "So far, it has been very rewarding and fun! I think Chennai is a big draw for a lot of people. It is certainly a big, old city with lots of cultural and social activities. And, of course, I do see challenges with infrastructure, crowds, pollution, and economic disparities. But people are nice and tolerant. I feel blessed to have friends like Abhi and Gai. And now, you all are being added to the list," he said, chuckling.

"Oh, wow, Robi. That's a perfect take on Chennai. We should meet more often," Anushya said with a charming smile.

As Gayatri's friends left, Robi and Gayatri settled the bill and prepared to head back. Gayatri calmly and warmly announced that she would drop Robi off and hailed an autorickshaw. They got in and made their way to Robi's service apartment, engaging in incessant conversation. Gayatri seemed more at ease, discussing her friends, family, college, and her future.

Robi was impressed by Gayatri's ability to process thoughts with tremendous clarity and articulate them lucidly. He felt himself increasingly drawn to her, sensing that their friendship was blossoming into something more. He decided to open up more to Gayatri and show that they should share their feelings for each other without holding back.

While these thoughts raced through his mind, Gayatri accompanied Robi to the corner, holding his hand while crossing the road to his apartment. "Thanks for joining us and being such a sport, Robi! You're comfortably getting into the thick of things in Chennai! Maybe you should learn more of the local lingo."

"You're so sweet, Gai! I've thoroughly enjoyed the time with you and your friends. I should thank you for inviting me," Robi replied.

"Oh, great! That was fun, right? Anyway, let me take an auto from the other corner. You take care and have a good night's sleep, Romeo."

"Oh, no! Am I getting notorious in Chennai now? Anyway, let me walk you up to the corner."

"Sounds good. Thanks, Robi. And, by the way, I wanted to know if you can attend my piano recital next week at my college. One of the leading music honchos will be presiding. I'm sure you won't be bored. Abhi and Janani might show up if they're free."

"Oh, okay. I'll be happy to tag along. Looking forward to that, Gai. See ya. Take care!" Robi bid farewell.

Whistling, Robi made his way back to his apartment, recollecting every minute spent with Gayatri. The feeling was surreal! He felt things were happening too fast but in the right direction. He was gradually coming to understand what it meant to love someone and be drawn to them in a nice, caring way. This was a feeling he had never experienced before. He couldn't wait to talk to his parents about it.

Chapter 21

Hope in Desperation

It was the perfect time for Robi to call his parents in Los Angeles. Dialing their home number, he caught them during their morning coffee time. His parents were in a relaxed and happy mood as they heard their son's voice.

Robi had always felt comfortable discussing personal matters with his parents. He could freely talk about almost anything with them. They were thrilled, as always, to hear from their only child. After the usual exchange of greetings and pleasantries, Robi eagerly shared the latest turn of events in his life.

"Mom, Dad, I have some exciting news for you. You won't believe it... I think I'm falling in love with an amazing person here in Chennai. I'm not kidding, Mom, Dad! It's happening!" Robi exclaimed.

Robi provided all the details about the unfolding events in Chennai, and after a brief moment of silence, his father was the first to respond.

"Wow, that's welcome news, son! We're elated to hear this!" his father expressed.

"We're thrilled, honey. How did it all happen so fast?" his mother asked with genuine curiosity.

"It's exciting, son, but remember to do what feels right for you. We're here to support you," his father added, injecting a lot of emotion into the long-distance call.

After some parental advice on how to approach the situation, Robi's parents bid him goodbye and promised to call him later.

Feeling charged up and reassured by his parents' support, Robi looked forward to spending more time with Gayatri. The only challenge now was to find out her feelings towards him.

Robi didn't want to miss any opportunity to be with Gayatri. He joined Abhi and Janani to attend the piano recital at her college. Gayatri's 45-minute performance was breathtaking. Her dexterous handling of the keys and fluent rendition left the audience in awe.

After the recital, all three of them went on stage and hugged Gayatri, praising her remarkable performance in front of the audience. It was a heartwarming moment shared among friends and family.

Robi and Gayatri started meeting regularly, both at the office and at Gayatri's favorite coffee shop, Amethyst. They liked shopping together, watching movies, and meeting friends. Gayatri felt increasingly comfortable in Robi's presence and took it upon herself to teach him the local language, Indian-style cooking, and the way of life in Chennai. Robi found himself drawn to the beauty of the local culture and language, and he often sought Gayatri's opinion on various matters.

Meanwhile, at the GOLI office, Abhi and Robi were deeply involved in taking the company to the next level. Abhi praised Robi for his business acumen and his ability to quickly adapt to the local culture.

"You're getting right into the thick of things, Robi. Not only are you showing great business skills, but everyone is thoroughly impressed with how you've embraced the local culture. You're becoming a true Chennai boy!" Abhi exclaimed gleefully.

"Thanks to Gai, man! She's been patiently teaching me all the nuances, and though it's not easy, I'm getting there," Robi replied with an impish grin.

"Alright, let's get things moving here," Abhi said, filled with excitement.

The GOLI team put the work on fast track, preparing for a ceremonial Diwali launch. As October began, Robi, Abhi, and the team geared up to roll out the beta site and start transactions on October 15th, just before Diwali, the most popular festival in India.

With some minor hiccups along the way, the GOLI team successfully launched their powerful e-commerce site and made marketing plans to attract visitors. Though the transactions started slowly, they never ceased, and the outsourced fulfillment team stayed busy handling orders.

In the midst of it all, Abhi's parents decided to host a gala Diwali celebration, marking an important event for the newly married couple. Robi and the entire GOLI team were invited, and Robi eagerly anticipated the vibrant Diwali festivities at Abhi's place.

As expected, the celebration organized by Abhi's parents was top class and showcased the rich cultural aspects of the festival. Robi learned a great deal about Indian traditions and customs. Gayatri, in her elegant manner, delivered yet another musical performance for Janani and Abhi celebrating their first Diwali together.

Gayatri made sure she introduced Robi to people he hadn't met before, leaving a deep impact on him. His feelings towards Gayatri grew exponentially.

Robi had made up his mind. He was willing to invest all the time necessary to be with Gayatri and find the right moment to express his love for her. He wanted to move forward and ask her to be his life partner, even though it felt risky and things were happening rapidly. His parents' unwavering support served as his motivation, and he found himself calling them almost every other day.

A few days after the Diwali holidays, Robi decided to open up more to Gayatri. Encouraged by his parents and inspired to express his affection in a cultured and positive manner, he wanted to lavish her with attention.

"Be a Roman in Rome and embrace their way of life, son. Respect their culture and traditions. You will succeed, no matter the obstacles," his parents had advised. That evening, after the phone call, Robi cried tears of joy, feeling the immense strength his parents' words provided.

Parents can either strengthen or weaken one's conviction and beliefs when it comes to matters of love. Robi was fortunate to have his parents' steadfast support. He hoped that Gayatri's parents would be equally open-minded and approve of his love for their daughter. However, he worried about their mindset, wondering if they would prioritize cultural nuances and be able to go beyond predetermined boundaries.

In the same vein, Gayatri began to develop positive feelings towards Robi. While she couldn't fully comprehend the situation yet, she was captivated by his warmth and care. He consistently proved to be a kind-hearted gentleman with a solid mind, unlike the men she had encountered before. Although everything felt like a whirlwind and moved too fast, she couldn't deny that Robi was on her mind every night before she went to bed.

Robi had taken the decision to pursue his feelings for Gayatri wholeheartedly. He was prepared to invest the necessary time and effort to be with her and hoped to find the right moment to fully open up. Despite the practicalities, cultural differences, and the mindset of those around them, he was determined to make it work. The journey felt rather precarious, but his conviction pushed him forward.

Chapter 22

Blossoming Dreams

Robi wasted no more time in wooing Gayatri. They spent their days hanging out at malls, restaurants, and watching movies—a dream come true for Robi. He decided it was time to confess his love and immediately made plans for a formal dinner date at the posh Dakshin restaurant in the nearby Park Sheraton Hotel. Gayatri eagerly accepted the invitation and got dressed up for their meeting at the classy restaurant.

The dinner setting was formal, but Robi's cool demeanor and graceful communication skills made Gayatri feel at ease. They talked about various topics, including Robi's conversation with his parents.

"It's so sweet of them to encourage you like that, Robi. I'm really liking what's happening between us. I care deeply for you, but..." Gayatri's voice trailed off.

Robi promptly reached out and held her hand. "I have to say, Gai, that I tremendously enjoy being with you. I like everything about you—your intelligence, wit, talent, and, of course, your captivating personality."

He hesitated for a moment and then continued, "I am in love with you, Gai. You are very special to me, and without a doubt, you are the person for me! I've been waiting for this day to open up to you."

"I am in love with you too, Robi!" Gayatri professed.

Robi's heart skipped a beat at her words.

"But I'm scared. It's all happening so fast. Over the past few days, many thoughts have been crossing my mind—my parents, the cultural differences as they might see it... it's scary, Robi," Gayatri expressed her concerns.

"I understand, Gai. I've thought about all of these many times. Believe me, I don't commit easily. I've spent ample time with you to get to know you very well. I am sure you are the one for me, and there's no doubt in my mind. I believe it's meant to happen. As they say, destiny has brought me here for a special reason— to find the love of my life. I won't coerce you into this, Gai, but my feelings are real, and things between us have gone beyond friendship... don't you think?" Robi reassured her.

Gayatri became emotional and tearful. "Yes, Robi. I want to be with you, Robi, but we have to convince my parents too..."

"Sure, Gai. I will do anything for you. I appreciate your concern for your parents. It's important. Rest assured, we'll do it the Indian way," Robi promised.

"Yes, we have to seek everyone's blessings, Robi."

"True, Gai! You are my girl," smiled Robi, planting a gentle kiss on her cheek.

After much deliberation, Gayatri decided to discuss the situation with Abhi and inform him that her relationship with Robi had evolved beyond friendship and that they had true feelings for each other.

After patiently listening to Gayatri's fast-paced tale, Abhi remained unusually calm for a long time before finally saying, "I am caught off-guard here, Gai. This has escalated way too fast! I never expected Robi to commit to something like this so quickly. He's a genuine guy, and of course, a close friend of mine, but I need time to digest this. Maybe the three of us can talk together?"

Gayatri felt immensely relieved that Abhi was now aware of their relationship and willing to help them navigate through this situation.

A few days later, the three of them met and openly discussed their unique love story.

"Wow, it's hard to believe what's happening here, guys! You've taken me by surprise. I didn't expect you to be the "settling down" type, Robi!" exclaimed Abhi.

"Hey, Abhi! I should have opened up to you earlier, man. Sorry! I wanted to discuss this with Gai first... but yeah, things are moving fast, dude. Even I thought I wouldn't want to settle down this early. Gai here has swept me off my feet, man. Seriously!" said Robi, gently hugging Gayatri.

"Well, I'm thrilled for you guys. I have to admit, I'm not sure how to react or advise, but handle this with the utmost care, especially with Gai's parents. But I'm on your side, lovebirds," responded Abhi with a big smile.

"We have a plan for that, Abhi. Thanks for being so encouraging, man!" Robi said, his eyes filled with tears.

With Gayatri's consent and Abhi's support, Robi decided to call his parents and ask them to visit Chennai to formally ask for Gayatri's hand in marriage, following Indian traditions. Once both families agreed, they would have a formal engagement ceremony.

Chapter 23

Stepping into the Unknown

It was relatively easy for Robi to convince his parents to come over and participate in the formalities, although he felt a twinge of guilt about inconveniencing them. The two fifty-five-year-olds, at the peak of their careers, had to travel on short notice to a distant land. However, Robi hoped that they would win the hearts of everyone, especially Gayatri's parents.

Feeling nervous about the situation, Robi called Abhi to discuss their chances of success.

"Hi, Robi! You've made up your mind, and Gai is fully onboard. So why the cold feet now? Just go for it. Bring your parents over. I'll make arrangements for them to stay at the Park," said Abhi.

"Thanks, Abhi. I don't know what to say, man. You're right. Everything is happening so fast. But I'm really in love, buddy! Gai is special to me. I don't want to let her down, and that's why I'm nervous," Robi confessed.

"Don't worry, Robi. My parents are surprised too, but they're happy for you. We'll arrange a meeting between both sets of parents at our place. Just get the ball rolling, dude," reassured Abhi.

"Abhi, look at where destiny has taken me, man. First, I met you, and then your cousin sister, Gai... I feel so immensely blessed!" Robi said, his eyes welling up with tears of joy.

"It's meant to happen, Robi. Let's get ready for it," Abhi assured him.

Robi and Gayatri made the necessary preparations to receive Robi's parents. Once again, it was Vetri, the driver, who took them to the Chennai airport. The ride was unusually calm, with both Robi and Gayatri lost in their thoughts. Gayatri was particularly anxious, knowing that her parents were unaware of the progression of their relationship. She was a bit delirious about preparing her parents, and decided to go with the flow and hoped for the best outcome. She trusted Robi's commitment and was grateful for Abhi's support.

It was a pleasant November evening in Chennai, with a gentle breeze blowing and no signs of heavy rains. Gayatri held a bouquet in one hand and Robi's hand in the other as they waited to welcome Robi's parents, who were visiting India for the first time ever. The atmosphere was filled with romance as they eagerly anticipated their arrival.

When Robi's parents walked out of the airport, pushing a trolley and confidently navigating the unfamiliar surroundings, Robi couldn't contain his excitement.

"Welcome, Mom and Dad! I'm so happy to see you!" Robi greeted them emotionally, hugging them tightly. "And here is the lovely Gai!"

"Oh my God, you are so beautiful, Gai! We're thrilled to meet you," exclaimed Robi's parents as they warmly embraced her and accepted the bouquet.

"Welcome to Chennai. We're delighted to have both of you here. How was the journey?" asked Gayatri, engaging in a conversation with Robi's parents.

The conversation continued as they made their way to the car and headed to the hotel. Gayatri quickly warmed up to Robi's parents and developed an instant liking for them. They exuded grace and affection.

At the hotel, they were joined by Abhi. It was time to discuss the meeting between the two sets of parents. It was a rather unusual way of going about things, but it had to be done.

Abhi's parents arranged the meeting between the Bascoms and the Ranjans at their luxurious residence, as per Abhi's request. The Bascoms, along with Robi, entered the house gracefully after removing their shoes at the entrance. Greetings were exchanged, and the gifts brought by the Bascoms from the United States were accepted.

Abhi's father served drinks and set up the cocktail plates. However, Gayatri's parents, the Ranjans, chose not to indulge in cocktails. They appeared concerned about the suddenness of the meeting and pressed Gayatri for answers, to which she evasively responded.

The Kumars ensured that everyone felt at ease and got to know each other. The younger generation sipped their drinks in silence, eagerly awaiting the main interaction.

Dr. Malcolm Bascom, Robi's father, expressed his appreciation for Chennai and expressed immense gratitude to the Kumars for taking care of their son.

He jokingly said, "I am so happy to be here with my wife, Maggie. She swept me off my feet thirty years ago, and she hasn't allowed me to look at any other women!" Laughter filled the room, breaking the ice. "And Robi has made our family complete," he continued.

Dr. Bascom, now in the spotlight, began his grand gesture. The scotch served by Kumar helped him loosen up.

"Well, everyone, if I may... I want to say that we have experienced the same attraction that Robi is feeling here in Chennai—the power of love. It happened to Maggie and me, and it is an incredibly strong force," Dr. Bascom eloquently stated.

"This is one of those rare occasions when Maggie lets me give a speech all by myself," he added, generating more laughs and smiles. Janani, Abhi, Gayatri, and Abhi's parents were thoroughly impressed.

Maggie chimed in, "Oh, wait a minute, Malcolm, that's not true. You always like to talk!" Her loving nudge elicited more smiles. Robi beamed with pride as he looked at his parents.

Dr. Bascom regained everyone's attention, "I need to get to the point and ask for your permission and acceptance to have sweet Gai join our family. Robi and Gai have openly expressed their love for each other and wish to become life partners. Maggie and I wholeheartedly support them, and it would be an honor to witness them leading a happy and joyful life. Yes, it may have happened quickly, but love knows no obstacles!" Dr. Bascom's eyes welled up with tears as he paused.

A silence filled the living room. Gayatri's father appeared nervous, staring sternly at Gayatri and avoiding eye contact with Robi.

"Not sure what's happening here. We thought Robi and Gai were just friends. This shouldn't be taken lightly. We are not prepared for this, Dr. Bascom," Ranjan responded.

He then turned to Kumar and Abhi, directly asking if they were aware of the situation.

Robi shook his head in despair and looked helplessly at a teary-eyed Gayatri. Dr. Bascom stepped forward to ease the tension.

"Mr. Ranjan and everyone here, we also thought it was happening too fast. But deep down, our children are truly in love... I'm shedding tears of joy because our two beautiful kids have found a deeper meaning in life by being together! In my opinion, we shouldn't hinder such pure love, Sir!" Dr. Bascom pleaded.

Ranjan was bewildered and said, "Sir, you don't understand the cultural differences and practicalities involved in making this work between two continents..."

"I understand that there are differences and practical considerations, Mr. Ranjan. We've been fortunate in our careers, building wealth, and providing the best for Robi, including teaching him to respect other cultures. Moreover, we live in an interconnected world where love transcends cultural and religious boundaries. We must embrace and respect the thought process of these two remarkable individuals who truly care for each other. And the fact that they invited us here to seek your approval is worth a ton of gold!" Dr. Bascom's eyes glistened again with tears.

He continued, "Gai means a lot to my son. He has embraced the Indian way of life in many aspects, thanks to Gai! We won't force you or them into anything, but our actions shouldn't lead to broken hearts and damaged friendships. Please, consider this sincerely—from the bottom of my heart!"

"Maggie always wanted a daughter after Robi, but nature denied us that. Now, nature is redeeming it through Gai. We have no ulterior motives, except to see our children happy," Dr. Malcolm concluded, placing his hand over his heart. Maggie and Gayatri couldn't contain their emotions.

Gayatri's father replied with an indifferent tone, "Well, Gai is our only daughter, and we must be cautious in guiding her, Sir. This has caught us by surprise. Please, we are not quite ready for this," he seemed prepared to leave abruptly.

Kumar finally intervened, saying, "Dr. Bascom and Maggie, I suggest we allow Gayatri's parents time to reflect on the situation. Let's proceed with dinner and take the opportunity to get to know each other better."

The meeting between the parents reached a stalemate, leaving Robi deeply disturbed by the entire episode. He couldn't comprehend the parochial approach to marriage and the possessiveness of the parents. Although unfamiliar with such sentiments, he decided to remain steadfast for Gayatri.

As they bid farewell, Robi defiantly held Gayatri's hand and assured her that she was the only one for him. Period.

Chapter 24

The Long Night

Gayatri returned home with overwhelming sadness and trepidation; emotions unfamiliar to her within the walls of her own home. Nevertheless, she was prepared to face her parents' anger and indifference.

It was nearing midnight, and Gayatri's father, Ashok Ranjan, sat on the couch in the hallway with an imperious look, ready to unleash his rage.

"Gayatri, sorry, but we need to talk. This is not what we expected from you. What is going on here? This is unthinkable and you are crossing the line. You should have discussed this with us before. You have really let us down," Ranjan ranted with mixed emotions.

"Your mother is extremely upset and in a state of confusion. Is it fair what you are doing to us? How can we allow this to happen before our eyes? You are our only child, and we want the best for you. This is not what we had in mind, and we can't accept it," he continued.

Gayatri composed herself and mustered an unprecedented courage to defend herself and assert her right to be with the person she loved and who genuinely cared for her.

"I know I made a terrible mistake of not discussing this earlier with you. But the world is changing, Appa, Amma. Is wholehearted love a sin? Can't you see the sincerity in our relationship? What is wrong with Robi? He is well-educated, comes from a great family, and embodies culture, refinement, and responsibility. I have considered all the consequences and even agreed to have Robi's parents over," Gayatri reasoned.

"But, Gai, dear, don't confuse friendship with love!" her mother interjected, her voice filled with emotion.

"Well, I am old enough to make the right decision, Amma. You and Appa have always stood by me. Why take such a hard stance without giving any credence to our feelings? It seems like any amount of rational talk won't help here," Gayatri said, starting to sob. "So, if marriage is off the table for me, so be it. But my friendship with Robi will continue, and I am not in the frame of mind to consider anyone else."

Gayatri stormed out of the room, deciding not to engage in further discussion with her parents. She sought her own space and decided to focus her energy on exploring other opportunities, such as pursuing higher education.

Abhi found himself tasked with a delicate and highly sensitive request from his uncle Ranjan. Ashok Ranjan, without directly blaming Abhi for the burgeoning problem, poignantly asked him to talk to both Robi and Gayatri, hoping to convince Robi to back out of his involvement with Gayatri.

Abhi did his best to convince his uncle and aunt about the relationship that Robi and Gayatri shared and why they should reconsider their stance on the matter. However, Ranjan responded firmly, with pent-up anger in his voice.

"This is too much to accept, Abhi. I won't reconsider my stance on this outrageous and farcical love. It's impractical. Please understand. Just talk some sense into your friend. That's all we're asking. I'm begging you, Abhi," Ranjan pleaded.

"Oh no, uncle. This situation is too stressful and unusual for me to deal with. How can you expect me to hurt the feelings of the two people I care for so deeply?" Abhi replied.

"Okay then, Abhi! It's tough for me to say this, but we cannot proceed with this marriage and witness our only child deviating so drastically from our cultural roots. I think if we put a stop to it, this so-called impractical love will fade away!" Ranjan retorted emphatically, catching Abhi by surprise.

"Uncle, please understand that moving in this direction is also a huge risk. We can't dictate terms. Both Robi and Gai know what they're doing. Can you think it over? Times are changing," Abhi pleaded.

Finally, Abhi's aunt intervened dramatically, exhorting, "Well, Abhi, this is unthinkable! How can we accept this? We don't feel good about it. Please, we beg you to put an end to this."

Unable to bear witnessing his aunt's incessant sobbing, Abhi felt the need to leave the scene. All he could muster was, "I can only talk to them," as he walked away, consumed by anguish. He found himself caught between a rock and a hard place.

A day after the dramatic events and a torrent of emotions, Abhi knocked on Robi's door. Heavy rain poured outside, and the dark clouds overhead created an intense atmosphere. It was an ominous situation, and Abhi knew it.

"Hey, come on in, Abhi! Quite a surprise, dude. So, what's going on, man?" Robi welcomed him with a sense of resentment.

"Hi, Robi! I want to apologize for what happened yesterday. I expected some initial resistance, but not this stubborn stance from Gai's parents. I am utterly distraught, man! I have no idea how to handle this situation," Abhi confessed.

"Listen, Abhi, I can't walk away from my commitment to Gai. I truly love her, man. I'm serious, dude. Why all this fuss and drama? What's wrong with people? It's the twenty-first century!" Robi exclaimed.

"I understand, Robi. This situation is terrible, man. My family is old-fashioned, and I should have warned you earlier. But I was hopeful and wanted the best for you and Gai," Abhi explained.

"Okay, man! Let's be real here. I can't give up on Gai. My love and commitment are unwavering and absolute. What do you want me to do? Are you still on my side?" Robi questioned.

"Yes, Robi. I was taken aback when Gai's father asked me to talk you out of this. I pleaded with him to change his mind, but the old man won't budge. Please don't lose sleep over this, okay? You, me, and Gai can discuss it later this evening," Abhi suggested.

"No way, Abhi! Let's call Gai and talk right now, man. I don't want Gai to suffer any longer. I need to see her," Robi insisted fervently.

Gai was driven to Eliot's Beach by Vetri, thanks to Abhi's efforts. The three individuals, bound closely by their friendship, met in a secluded area where they wouldn't be seen or heard by others.

Robi embraced Gai tightly, apologizing profusely for not handling the situation well.

Gai, with tears streaming down her face, said, "It's not your fault at all, Robi. Please don't apologize. I think my parents are blowing the whole thing out of proportion. Also, I should have prepared them a little better."

Abhi gently interjected, "Listen, guys. We need to think calmly and objectively about this."

"Well, Abhi, how can we be calm when everything is falling apart? You know me—I don't commit easily. I deeply love and care for Gai, and I want to be with her, man. I'm serious now. It's Gai or nobody," Robi declared.

"Robi, just relax! Both of you are adults. Give it some time, and everything will fall into place," Abhi suggested.

"What do you mean, Abhi? Are you serious? Do you want me to give up? Is that what I'm hearing?" Robi shouted.

"Calm down, Robi! I'm not saying that. The family needs time. Right now, I can't convince them. Please understand," Abhi clarified.

"I hope you're not serious, Abhi. I'm devastated to hear you say that on behalf of the family. This is utter nonsense! Where is the true cultural open-mindedness? My parents have been insulted, dude. They accepted Gai with such grace and love. Why are they being turned away?" Robi expressed his frustration emphatically.

"Robi, you have to calm down and understand the situation here. We need time to bring them around. That's all I'm saying. You're taking it out of context," Abhi reasoned.

Robi became infuriated with Abhi's suggestion of buying time, and in a fit of rage, he lashed out at Abhi, saying, "You're full of it, Abhi! You could have stood up for us like a lion, but you didn't!"

"What's wrong with you, Robi? Have you been drinking too much? Just drop it, and let's discuss this later," Abhi retorted.

But Robi refused to back down, provoking Abhi to the point where the exchange of words grew fierce and spiraled out of control.

At that moment, Gai intervened, begging both of them to stop. Tears streaming down her face, she cried, "Please don't fight. I beg both of you not to fight because of me. It will only hurt me more. I can't understand what's happening around me."

"Abhi, why don't people give any credence to our love? Robi is sincere and honorable in our relationship. He never took advantage of me, and he never will. Why should cultural differences be given such prominence when the whole world is changing?" Gai implored.

Numb, Abhi could only mumble, "Things are moving too fast here, Gai! I'm completely at a loss for words. Just give it some time, please."

Gai started sobbing uncontrollably and hugged Robi, trying to keep her composure. "Let's all go home peacefully, please. I beg you, Robi. Please don't lose your cool. Let's sort this out without hurting anyone."

Chapter 25

The Monsoon Depression

The monsoon season brought dark clouds and a sense of despair. The somber atmosphere seeped into the lives of three inseparable friends: Robi, Abhi, and Gai. All the joyous moments had come to a halt, and it was unimaginable.

Despite facing strong opposition from his parents, Gai made her way to Robi's service apartment. She knew she had to mend the broken bonds of friendship and convince her parents to understand the depth of her relationship.

Gai understood that her parents wouldn't easily change their stance, but she remained resolute in upholding the principles of love and the value of true friendships. She knew what was best for herself and those around her.

Gai arrived at Robi's place in an autorickshaw and gently knocked on his door. Robi's face lit up with delight as he welcomed her inside. He embraced her warmly, expressing concern for her journey through the rain.

"It's alright, Robi. I'm more worried about you. Being in a distant land and dealing with so much on your own must be tough," Gai said, showing her care and compassion.

Robi managed a smile upon hearing Gai's caring words, feeling blessed to have her as an angel in his life. He reassured her, saying, "I'm not troubled that much, Gai. I'm grateful for having found you here."

"Robi, I don't want your friendship with Abhi to suffer because of me. We are friends first and foremost. Let's handle this maturely," Gai expressed her concerns.

"Of course, Gai! I sincerely apologize for the outburst with Abhi. I lost control," Robi admitted, regretting his actions.

"What should we do, Gai? I can't leave you like this. I'm fully committed, and I want to build a life together—a life filled with love, just like my parents'. We shouldn't let anything disrupt that. We have to stay strong in our conviction," Robi expressed his heartfelt desires.

"Robi, first and foremost, I want your parents to feel reassured. Let's spend time with them and show them that we'll be fine. It's important for them to go back home in peace. Let's do that, Robi, for our sake," Gai pleaded.

"Sure, baby. By all means, spending time with them will make them even prouder of you. We will always have their blessings. Don't worry about that," Robi replied, embracing Gai and inviting her to stay for lunch.

"Robi, please make amends with Abhi. He hasn't been returning my calls, and he's deeply hurt. I also want you to stay and help him with the business. You both shouldn't give up on your dreams," Gai requested.

"Well, maybe I let my emotions get the better of me and crossed a line. I'm sorry about that, Gai. Let's deal with this situation patiently. I'm shaken and distraught, not knowing how else to handle this. Let's do it your way since you understand the dynamics better," Robi conceded.

Robi requested his parents to come over and spend as much time as possible at his service apartment. Dr. Bascom and Maggie wasted no time in visiting their son's apartment, which was just a mile away. They were overjoyed to see Robi and Gai holding hands and warmly welcoming them with hugs and tears. Gai became emotional and started sobbing, expressing her apologies, "I am so sorry about what happened, Doc and Maggie. People just don't seem to understand how much I care about Robi or that we are in love."

Dr. Bascom gestured for Gai to sit next to him and reassured her, "Listen, dear. You are part of our family and always will be. Please have no doubts about that. We may not have accomplished our mission, but you have validated the sincerity of your commitment to each other."

Maggie added, "Well, Gai, sweetheart, you will always hold a special place in our hearts, no matter what! We are not walking away from this. We are with you and Robi. Tell us what we should do, and we'll do everything in our power."

Robi, in an emotional state, responded, "Mom, Dad, you have done your absolute best for us. Your trip has not been in vain. You have won the heart of this lovely human being, Gai! She has brought out the best of emotions in me through true love and positive vibes. I have reciprocated as you have taught me. I know there will be a happy ending. We just have to bring people around."

Dr. Bascom spoke affectionately, saying, "Sure, son, you both are sincere, and the higher power will show the way. Stay positive and cheer up! We are always with you!"

"Finally, Gai dear, we are not leaving empty-handed. We have rightfully earned you as our daughter through Robi, and again you'll always be part of our family. Wishing you both the best!" Dr. Bascom assured them.

The Bascoms savored the meal quickly prepared by Gai and bid an emotional farewell.

The following day, they were driven to Chennai Airport by Vetri. Robi and Gai accompanied them to say their goodbyes. Abhi was conspicuously absent, but he had the courtesy to visit the Bascoms in their hotel room to bid them farewell and apologize for all the unpleasant events. The Bascoms did not take anything to heart. This cultural environment was new to them, and they decided to work through the complex cultural maze for the sake of their son.

It was a solemn goodbye for the Bascoms at the airport, with their final message being, "We hope to see you both in LA soon. Love you both. Take care!" They expressed their feelings with big hugs and waving of hands.

Gai and Robi drove back in silence, holding each other. Vetri was confused about the whole drama and was afraid to ask either of them about it.

Abhi was at the office, which had taken on a somber mood. He knew it would take time for Robi to regroup and get back to the office. Goks and Anoop sensed that something was seriously wrong since Robi had been missing for a few days, and Abhi was spending very little time at the office. However, the young engineers didn't have the courage to intrude. Instead, they focused on completing their assigned tasks.

Midweek, the Chennai monsoons continued relentlessly, worsening the already gloomy moods of the youngsters. Abhi was extremely concerned about the absence of Robi's charismatic leadership, which was causing a decline in team morale.

Abhi finally mustered the courage to call on Robi and see if they could handle things professionally. He decided to go over to Robi's apartment.

It was a real shock for Abhi to see Robi in such a disheveled state — with unkempt hair, an unshaven beard, and still in his nightwear.

"Hi, how is it going, Robi?" Abhi started cautiously, maintaining a distant tone.

"Well, sorry about the other day, man. This isn't like me, and I feel completely shattered. I feel like a loser, being taken for a ride in this terrible city."

"Okay, we've had enough exchange of words the other day, Robi. Let's cool it, man. I just want you to recover and pick up the pieces so that we can make everything work for you and all of us."

"I'm not sure, Abhi. My mind has been going through severe gyrations. This is seriously messed up. I need time. I don't feel like coming to the office for a while. I miss Goks and Anoop, but I don't want to interact with them in this state."

"We need to work this out, Robi. This business is a serious commitment. We are accountable to all the people involved..." Abhi tried to approach the situation professionally.

"Well, you didn't answer Gai's calls for the past few days. This is just too much, man!"

"Okay, fine, Robi. Let's not mix things up. We have to sort this out somehow. It's only fair to everyone," said Abhi.

"Here we go, man. So, we have to sort things out? Can you give it to me straight, Abhi? Don't beat around the bush, man."

"No, we have to talk, Robi. You need to come to the office. It's good for you and all of us," said Abhi.

"Okay, now you're acting like the boss. I never expected this, Abhi. You're in your territory, man. That's what's making you talk like this. It's too much!" Robi expressed his frustration.

Abhi shook his head and said, "Come on, Robi. That hurts. I have always treated you like a friend, always!"

After a brief pause, Robi said, "Well, Abhi, sorry, man! I'm just extremely stressed out and blurting out like a madman. Please let me call you later, man."

Abhi left the apartment distraught and walked into the rain, feeling lost and confused.

Robi called Abhi the next day, as promised. "I wish things had not turned out so bad for me, Abhi! I've done everything the right way and followed all the protocols. So why is everything falling apart?"

"Listen, Robi! I have been straightforward about the reality. I supported you wholeheartedly and will continue to do so. You know that. You have to understand the perspective of the elders and patiently bring them to our side. That's how it works here, and I'm sure you've grasped that by now."

"Okay, but this is too much for me to handle. People getting in the way of how we want to live. I'm not sure, man! It's too bizarre for me. They've taken away my passion, my enthusiasm — my entire spirit has been crushed. I had so much going with you, Gai, Anoop, Goks, and our startup here... I don't know how to respond to your request, Abhi."

"Okay, Robi! Let's come up with a plan. What do you suggest we do to get you back on track?"

"I need time to regroup here. As you can see, I'm a total wreck, man. I want to regain my mental stability and ensure that Gai also recovers her cheerful self. Maybe I can be an advisor until I'm fully ready, but it's going to take time, man!" Robi expressed his melancholy.

"Well, we've come this far together. This is a serious business, Robi! We have stakeholders, a team, and customers! How can you step back for such a long time? Please come back, Robi, for everyone's sake! For all the effort we've put in!"

"I'm sorry, Abhi, but it's better for me to leave the company and the country, at least for now. I need to be away, probably with my parents, for a while."

Abhi was deeply stressed, contemplating the repercussions of Robi's departure. Their conversation escalated into another heated argument. Abhi was terribly perturbed and unable to control his emotions.

"Sorry, Robi! I got carried away. I'm deeply distressed by all this, man. It's starting to affect our friendship and the business, and I'm in a mess too, you know?"

"We're not seeing eye to eye anymore, Abhi. Let me stay away, man. I wish you all the best. Give my love to Goks and Anoop. I'll always be there for them." With those final words, Robi hung up the phone and decided to escape the sea of melancholy and distress.

Abhi was not a happy camper and just broke down. He felt that Robi could have handled the situation more calmly and remained committed to the business. Nevertheless, he was determined to preserve their deep-rooted friendship at any cost, for the sake of Gayatri as well.

Chapter 26

Miles Apart, Hearts Together

It was a chilly December morning, and the bustling city of Chennai was gearing up for what Gayatri referred to as the biggest cultural and music expo in India—the *Margazhi* Season. With a sizable Christian population, the city was also preparing for the Christmas festive season. The malls were adorned with Christmas trees and lights, offering various Christmas specials imported from Robi's homeland.

However, Robi was not in a celebratory mood. All he wanted was to have Gayatri by his side and spend as much time as possible with her. He asked her to come over so they could discuss their next course of action.

Gayatri gladly accepted the invitation, eager to leave her house and spend more time with Robi. She took an autorickshaw to Robi's apartment, a journey she had made countless times before. Robi rushed downstairs as soon as he heard the clunky autorickshaw noise. Overjoyed, he embraced Gayatri in broad daylight, much to the disapproval of conservative passersby. Gayatri didn't care about the opinions of others. She was in love, and nothing could change that.

Robi escorted Gayatri upstairs and offered her some juice to cool down, doing everything he could to make her comfortable. Despite the sudden turn of events and his feeling of helplessness, Gayatri managed to smile and lighten the somber atmosphere, teasing Robi about his well-grown stubble and carefree dressing.

"Looks like you're ready to join an ashram, my dear!"

"Oh, if you're going, I'm ready to follow you, baby. Maybe that would help us cool things down," they both burst into laughter after a long time.

Finally gathering the courage, Robi revealed to Gayatri that he was leaving for California during Christmas to clear his mind and figure out how they could overcome the obstacles with her parents.

"I hate leaving you alone here, Gai! But if I don't change the scenery, I'll become even more distressed. Besides, I had to tell Abhi that I can no longer continue in the business. It wouldn't be fair to him and the stakeholders. I'm just not in the right frame of mind, Gai. I'm overwhelmed with grief and confusion."

Robi noticed that Gayatri had tears in her eyes. He held her close and said, "I would love to take you with me, Gai! But it would complicate things further. I want you to come and join me on your own terms. I urge you to consider taking up a course or training in California. We need to approach this situation rationally and practically. Please plan on coming to the US. That's where we belong, baby. Please do this for me. Will you?"

At that moment, Gayatri sobbed uncontrollably. "I understand your feelings and what you need to do, Robi. Please don't forget about me. Empathize with my situation and emotions. Being a woman, it's tough, Robi!"

Robi choked up, his voice heavy with emotion. "That will never happen, Gai. You are the only one for me. I will never leave you. I promise once again—you are the only one for me! I want to be with you and build a family together, Gai. I'm serious, man. You have to be brave and join me as soon as possible."

"Will you do that, Gai? Please assure me. What else do I need to do? I want both of us out of this mess. Let's handle it calmly and get everyone on board. We can't resort to foolish actions that would only make things worse!"

Gayatri hugged Robi tightly, as if she would never let go of him.

"Let things cool off, Robi. I'm confident that I can devise a strategy that will benefit everyone. Let's deal with this sensibly. I believe good things are waiting for us."

Robi and Gayatri decided to cook lunch together and discuss the logistics of Robi's trip. Cooking together and reminiscing about their happy times in Chennai helped them relax, and soon, they were all smiles.

Thanks to one of Gayatri's travel agent friends, Robi managed to secure a ticket to LAX during the peak Christmas season. However, he couldn't shake off the pain of leaving Gayatri behind. She was an angel and a perfect fit for him and his family. Robi focused on regaining his confidence so that he could instill the same in Gayatri and make every effort to bring her to the US. He explored various opportunities for her, determined to find the best path for Gayatri.

Robi wasn't just in love with Gayatri; he was also in awe of her dynamism and quick thinking. She assisted Robi with packing, last-minute shopping, and vacating the service apartment.

Robi informed his parents about his decision to spend Christmas with them. They were happy to hear that he was coming, but couldn't hide their disappointment that Gayatri wouldn't be accompanying him. Vetri was once again entrusted with the task of driving Robi to the airport, thanks to Gayatri obtaining permission from her aunt. Vetri gladly accepted the opportunity to spend time with the young couple. Though he wasn't as worldly as the people he worked for, he recognized Robi's nice qualities and felt that he deserved to be with Gayatri, who had shown immense love and affection for him. Vetri refrained from discussing the troubling situation but was saddened to see Robi leaving Chennai in a somber mood, far from his usual humorous self. He knew that things had gone terribly wrong.

Vetri drove the Innova to Robi's Service Apartment along with Gayatri. Goks and Anoop met Robi at his apartment and helped him load the bags into the car. Robi hugged them both, and accepted the parting gifts they gave him. His final words were, "Thanks for everything, Goks and Anoop. You guys are just amazing man!. Please stick with Abhi and assist him. You can always count on me for anything. Come visit me in the US, champs."

"Thank you so much, Robi," Goks and Anoop said in unison.

"We'll miss you, Robi," Goks added, his voice soft and melancholic.

"Adios, amigos. I'm sure we'll meet again in happier times, guys. Take care of Gai for me. Will you?" Robi made a solemn request.

"Sure thing," Goks replied, with Anoop nodding his head, unable to conceal the sadness that had tainted what could have been a beautiful ending.

Gayatri watched the farewell scene unfold in silence, taking in the authentic warmth and goodwill Robi had built with so many people in Chennai. She felt disappointed and saddened by Abhi's decision not to go to the airport to bid farewell to his closest friend. Janani, too, felt uneasy being in the company of people in such a difficult state. She hoped for better times and sent Robi a beautiful silk kurta as a farewell gift. The Kumars conveyed their best wishes to Robi over the phone and asked him to visit Chennai again. They decided not to interfere in the matter, maintaining a diplomatic stance due to their family ties and allegiances.

Robi's drive to the airport was filled with mixed emotions. Only Gayatri accompanied him on this journey. This particular route to the airport had changed his life in unimaginable ways. When he had first set foot in this colorful city, he had anticipated a grand excursion. However, destiny had something else in store for him: the lovely Gayatri. He wanted to carry with him those wonderful memories of falling in love with someone so incredibly special, intelligent, and beautiful. In fact, she was sitting right next to him, holding his hand and putting up a brave front.

Robi was increasingly confident that Gayatri had a plan of her own, devised in her ingenious and thoughtful way. He became more certain that she would soon join him in the States. His conviction grew stronger by the minute, and he was determined to do whatever it took to bring his beloved to his homeland.

Robi decided to break the eerie silence in the car.

"Hi, Gai! Let's cheer up. I know it's just a matter of time. I want you to join me in the States. You should pursue your graduate studies in California. We can be closer there and work with our families to find a calm and practical solution."

"Well, why should I worry when you're so deeply committed to this, Robi? I'm sure things will work out. Everything happens for a reason. I believe we'll get through this phase and, in fact, strengthen our resolve."

"That's so sweet, Gai! You're incredibly strong, and I consider myself lucky to have you," Robi trailed off, not saying anything more, and noticed tears welling up in Gayatri's eyes.

Robi was speechless for a few minutes. He then shifted his attention to Vetri, who had been a fantastic friend and travel companion. As the Innova approached the airport terminal, in a highly emotional moment, Robi removed the watch he was wearing and asked Vetri if he would accept his Seiko watch as his token of appreciation.

Vetri didn't say anything at first. When he pulled the car over to the terminal curbside, he mentioned that the gift was too expensive.

As always, Robi persisted. "Please take this as my appreciation for all you have done, bro Vetri. I know you'll cherish it for life. I'm doing this in front of Gai, so she can vouch for you if someone suspects anything."

With tears flowing uncontrollably, Vetri accepted the precious gift and held Robi's hand for a moment. "Come back, Robi Sir!" he managed to say amidst his overwhelming emotions.

Now it was Gayatri's turn to hug Robi. "I'll terribly miss you, Robi! I'll join you soon. Please hang in there. Call me, text me often. Send my regards to your parents. I love them dearly!" Tears streamed down her face like a torrent.

Robi held Gayatri tightly for a good five minutes, oblivious to his surroundings. "You're the one for me, Gai. Let there be no doubt! I'll wait for you, baby, no matter how long it takes. Take care. Stay bold and cheerful, as always! See you soon."

With great difficulty, Robi bid farewell, holding back his tears, and ventured into the crowd, heading towards his home land. He was sad to be going alone, but he knew it was just a temporary obstacle in their journey together.

Part III: California, USA

Chapter 27

From Tears to Resilience

The Singapore Airlines flight touched down at LAX on time. Robi reminisced about the entire trip—the grand wedding of Abhi, trips to Mahabs, fun times with Abhi, dinners and lunches with Gai, his parents' visit, the startup with Abhi and the two young techies, and the affection from the Kumars, Vetri, Abhi, Janani, and Gai's friends.

Despite feeling fortunate, Robi was extremely distraught about his falling out with Abhi, which could have been avoided. Given the circumstances, he believed it was best for both of them to have some space.

During the trip, it was the time spent with his dear Gai that kept him tremendously buoyant. Gayatri had come into his life like a blessing from heaven, and he was still processing the positive emotions and love that had consumed him for the past several months. With that feeling of comfort, Robi disembarked from the plane and made his way back to his hometown.

Robi's parents were delighted to see him return but noticed the sadness in his eyes. They couldn't hide their disappointment that Gayatri had been left behind.

"It's only temporary, Mom, Dad. Cheer up! Gai is much braver than you think. She will be here in the States soon. I will make it happen. I promise. I want my angel here, Mom, Dad!" Robi said, choking emotionally.

His parents hugged him tightly, assuring him of their support and commitment to bringing Gayatri to the United States.

"We are with you, Robi. You know that. Gai is like our daughter. We want her to be here just as much as you, son!" said Mr. Bascom affectionately.

Maggie, Robi's mother, tried to bring some normalcy to the situation. "Honey, I want you to cheer up and be strong. Take some rest and start meeting your friends soon. Go out, have fun, and tell them about Gai. Show them your confidence, baby. You are a Bascom!"

"Thanks, Mom and Dad, for everything. Love you guys! Let me catch up on some sleep," said a tired and jet-lagged Robi before crashing into his favorite bed.

After a day of rest at home, Robi resumed his workout routine and began calling his friends in LA and the Bay Area. Every conversation revolved around his newfound love, Gayatri. He called her regularly, spending more than an hour talking to her each day.

Gayatri exuded confidence and shared the news that she had started preparing for her GMAT and TOEFL tests. She requested Robi's assistance in applying to Berkeley, UCLA, and UC Davis, as she had decided to pursue an MBA or an equivalent program in Management Studies.

Robi was overjoyed when he learned that Gayatri was enthusiastic about getting admission into one of the California universities. He reached out to his contacts at the universities and started laying the groundwork for her application. He discovered that Gayatri still had enough time to apply for programs starting in the fall semester. Excitedly, he shared this development with his parents, who were equally thrilled.

Robi thoroughly enjoyed the Christmas season and holiday celebrations, catching up with relatives and friends. Everyone was eager to know about Gayatri and their plans together. Jokes and teasing lifted his spirits, and he particularly relished the idea of kidnapping Gayatri from India, suggested by his friends in good humor. His routine improved, and regular conversations with Gayatri kept him energized. The distance between them felt unbearable at times, but they consoled each other, knowing it would only be for a few months.

The New Year brought good fortune to Robi. He received a call from his friend in the Bay Area who had joined a successful e-commerce aggregation company in Mountain View. They informed him about an International Business Development Manager position that had just opened up and encouraged him to apply. Robi acted swiftly, seizing the opportunity. Within a week, he was called for an interview and asked to fly down to Mountain View. The interview with the talented leadership team went well, and Robi expressed his desire to head the International Business Development for the company. He got what he wanted and had no reservations about moving back to the Bay Area for another career opportunity.

Silicon Valley's charm had always mesmerized Robi. He admired its informal and no-nonsense approach to business and the speed at which things were executed. Upon joining the company, which was already performing exceptionally well, Robi wasted no time in formulating a well-thought-out plan to expand into the global market. His experience in India proved invaluable.

Abhi heard from his Bay Area friends that Robi had joined a fast-growing e-commerce company in the Valley. He decided it was time to reach out to Robi and resolve their differences. However, Robi was not fully prepared and had yet to fully recover from the pain he had experienced. He postponed connecting with Abhi for a little longer.

In the meantime, upon the urging of his parents, Janani, and Gayatri, Abhi planned a trip to the Bay Area to meet with Robi and explore opportunities for his company in the US. He keenly felt Robi's absence at the office.

Spring had arrived in the sunny Bay Area, and Robi had taken up cycling and become addicted to it. He biked around nonchalantly, appreciating the scenery. While cycling near the picturesque Lakeshore area in Mountain View, he heard his iPhone buzzing incessantly. Though he didn't recognize the number, he decided to answer.

"Hi Robi, I wanted to surprise you. I just arrived here and I'm waiting for you at our favorite 'Tied House' on Castro Street!"

Robi instantly recognized the voice. In a somewhat casual tone, he replied, "Abhi! Are you in the area? When did you arrive?"

"I got here last night, Robi! Can we meet, please?" Abhi asked, almost pleading.

"Okay, man! This is way too unexpected, but I'll be there, Abhi. I have mixed feelings about many things. But, I'm happy to catch up," Robi responded diplomatically.

Abhi greeted Robi with a gentle hug at the Tied House, one of the liveliest sports bars in Mountain View. He had already settled down at a table with a pitcher of craft beer and chicken wings.

"Good to see you, Robi! We all miss you, man, especially Gai! My parents and Janani insisted that I meet with you and work things out for a smooth transition."

"Well, you did catch me by surprise, Abhi! How's Gai? Janani? Your parents?" Robi inquired.

"They're all doing well. Gai talks about you boldly and shares her plan to join you here for her graduate studies. In fact, I brought her application forms along with me to dispatch to the various universities," Abhi said calmly and optimistically.

"Thank you, man! As you know, I'm not in the mood to go back to Chennai right now. I've just started rebuilding my life. It has been tough, but Gai and my parents have been a major source of strength and inspiration. I absolutely want Gai to be here, and we'll sort everything out," Robi replied, his voice quivering with emotion.

"We're all behind you and Gai. Her parents are slowly turning around. It is quite encouraging on that front. But we also need you in Chennai to scale up the business. Goks and Anoop haven't been the same since you left. All our partners are asking for you. Please reconsider your decision, Robi, at least for a short while?" Abhi pleaded.

"I just started my job and life here, Abhi. I miss all the action over there. But, for now, I'm not changing any plans. Sorry, man! But, I'll do anything for GOLI from here. I promise!" Robi expressed with increased empathy.

"Okay. Let's discuss it further, Robi. I'm here for about a week. But before that, update me on what's been happening here."

The two friends ended up spending more time than expected and decided to meet again to figure out a way to help each other and, most importantly, bring Gai over to the States. Abhi was slightly disappointed that he couldn't convince Robi to return to Chennai to help with GOLI, but he remained optimistic about getting Robi's support to boost the business with partners and motivate Goks and Anoop. Robi suggested finding a young, energetic business development manager whom he could mentor.

Abhi was willing to accept any help as he was desperate to move forward. Although a couple of his friends had stepped in to assist temporarily, Robi was irreplaceable.

Robi strongly believed that he should reconcile with the past and restore the cherished friendship he had with Abhi. The two Stanford mates spent a lot of time on campus and in San Francisco, meeting with faculty members, undergraduate students, and friends. It was nostalgic and refreshing for both of them. The Bay Area would always hold its charm!

The two friends began reminiscing about the good times they had at Stanford. Abhi was even more impressed by Robi's transformation and charismatic personality, and believed Gai was lucky to have been captivated by such a remarkable person.

"Look how life has changed, Robi! The power of love has taken you to another level, man. In any case, I'm so proud of you. Gai is amazed by you. I think she's ready to come over here and be with you."

"Well, let's make it happen, Abhi. As I always told you, she is the best thing that has happened to me and my family. She's just perfect, man. Too perfect for me! She's the one for me, Abhi. No doubt, man! I'll wait for her and do whatever it takes to have her here," Robi said with a lump in his throat.

Abhi, without any hesitation, hugged him and assured him that he was tremendously delighted and would do everything within his capacity.

Robi agreed to drive Abhi to the SFO airport. On the way, he mentioned, "By the way, Abhi, my company is looking for a strategic technology and business partner in the Asia Pacific region. I want you to sign up and cover the region for us with your resources and platform. I'll send you all the details. It's a great opportunity, and since I'm in charge, I can expedite things for you."

"That's fantastic, Robi! It's a breakthrough, in my opinion. Sure, send me all the details. I'll review and sign up!"

Abhi said farewell to his dear friend at the same place he had met a few years back. He was emotional and was at a loss for words. He hugged Robi and thanked him for everything.

Robi waved his friend goodbye and asked him to pass on his hugs and kisses to Gayatri.

Chapter 28

The Great Leap

Robi realized how much he missed Abhi and reflected on the years they had spent together. He deeply regretted hurting Abhi's feelings in a fit of anger and wished it hadn't happened. He recognized that he had found the love of his life through Abhi and felt indebted to him. He was determined to do whatever it took to assist Abhi with his business.

As expected, Abhi signed a strategic partnership agreement with Robi's company to handle Business Processing and Support in the Asian region. The business structure was well-designed, leveraging the simple transactional technology that GOLI had already established in the region. Robi, along with Goks and Anoop, worked tirelessly to set up the infrastructure for e-commerce transactions and fulfillment through the GOLI platform. Within a few months, the partnership achieved remarkable targets, and Abhi was thrilled with the mutually beneficial arrangement.

Abhi spent significant time with Gayatri, explaining the details of the business arrangement and highlighting Robi's involvement in the operational aspects. She was overjoyed to learn that the two friends had reconciled and were working together enthusiastically. She decided to contribute by assisting with administrative tasks while also familiarizing herself with the business operations.

Motivated by the unwavering support of the two men she admired, Gayatri pushed forward with her plans. She applied to six universities, taking guidance from Robi and receiving support from Abhi to accelerate the process. She felt incredibly fortunate to have their backing in pursuing her educational goals.

Gayatri diligently completed the application process, with Robi submitting three applications on her behalf and assisting with a few online submissions through Abhi's guidance. In April, she received her aptitude test scores, surpassing expectations by achieving a high-percentile threshold. She felt immensely confident that she would get accepted into one of her top three choices among the UC schools.

Robi, eager to support Gayatri's aspirations, reached out to his contacts at UC Berkeley and UCLA to inquire about the status of her admission into their respective MBA programs. Around June, Robi received a text from his contact at the Haas School of Business in Berkeley, informing him that Gayatri Ranjan had been accepted and would soon receive the official letter. Overjoyed, Robi immediately shared the news with his parents, Gayatri, and Abhi. The following week, Gayatri also secured a spot on the final list of the UCLA MBA program.

Gayatri was doubly ecstatic to receive admission offers from her two preferred universities, both of which had been highly recommended by Robi and supported by Abhi. However, considering the proximity to Robi's workplace, she made the decision to attend UC Berkeley. She accepted the admission offer and proceeded to fulfill the necessary formalities, including obtaining a supplemental bank loan to cover the expenses, as she didn't want to burden her parents.

Abhi met with Gayatri multiple times to provide assistance with various procedural tasks such as applying for a student visa, securing a student loan, and handling other related matters.

Gayatri was overjoyed by the developments, but she also felt a tinge of sadness for not consulting her parents on certain decisions. Her parents gradually came to terms with her choice, understanding that she was committed to her educational and life goals. While Gayatri's father remained largely quiet, he congratulated her on her accomplishments and vowed to support her in any way he could. Her mother, though reluctant to let go of her only child, recognized her daughter's bravery and believed she would handle everything well in the United States. They didn't discuss Robi much and left it to Gayatri to decide the appropriate course of action. It wasn't an ideal situation for Gayatri, but she was grateful that time had healed some wounds.

Abhi played a pivotal role in empowering Gayatri and convincing her parents that she was on the right path and should be encouraged to pursue her MBA and plan her life accordingly. The Kumars, along with Janani, provided unflinching support throughout the time. They asserted that Gayatri is very level headed and will do only what is right. Gayatri's parents found comfort in such words and felt that they should respect the positive aspirations and wishes of their only child.

Robi was on cloud nine! His parents hosted a nice party at their Santa Monica home to commemorate Gayatri's admission into UC Berkeley. They arranged a video chat session for about an hour to express their joy and anticipation of having her in California. Robi now spoke with Gayatri multiple times a day to ensure that everything was progressing smoothly.

Without any hiccups, Gayatri's student visa was approved by the US consulate. It was a dream come true for her! She booked her flight to San Francisco and meticulously planned all the logistics, including shopping, packing, bidding farewell to her friends, and, most importantly, comforting her parents with love and affection. She wanted her parents to select the dresses for her and host farewell parties at home.

Gayatri announced that she would be departing on August 17th, 2010, to San Francisco—the same day Abhi had left for the US four years prior. Abhi couldn't help but feel sentimental about the events unfolding for his dear sister. It was difficult to believe that she would follow in his footsteps to the Bay Area and be welcomed by the same person who had greeted him and become his closest friend, soon to be a part of their close-knit family. Abhi was certainly engulfed by the whirlwind of events happening around him, but it was all moving in the right direction. Destiny had shaped their lives and family in unimaginable ways. He was overjoyed for Gayatri and immensely proud of Robi's resolute commitment and character in pursuing a relationship with her.

Vetri once again drove the family's Innova, followed by a large caravan of people, to the Chennai International Airport. This time, the atmosphere in the car was livelier, and Gayatri displayed signs of excitement mixed with emotions. Throughout the journey, she held her father's hand, expressing her deep love for him despite his reservations about her decisions. He remained in deep contemplation, cherishing the moment while tightly holding onto his beloved daughter—the light of his life! Gayatri's mother was in a happier mood, providing motherly advice and support.

Abhi couldn't help but think that all moms are the same.

At the airport, Gayatri received a fitting farewell from a large group of friends. Many bystanders wondered if a celebrity was leaving town. Gayatri reveled in the atmosphere and fought back tears, trying her best to stay composed. However, when her parents embraced her together, she lost all control and sobbed like a little kid.

"I will never let you down, Amma, Appa!"

Her words were soothing, filled with love and affection. It was a spontaneous message that parents yearn to hear from their children. Abhi was the last person to embrace her and bid her an emotional farewell.

Gayatri waved goodbye to all her friends and family members, slowly blending into the bustling airport and embarking on her journey toward greener pastures.

Chapter 29

The Reunion

Robi felt a wave of nostalgia and sentimentality as he drove his well-preserved Toyota Camry to SFO Airport to pick up the love of his life. It was the same place and time where he had met Abhi four years ago. It was a watershed moment in his life, a pivotal turning point that would forever shape his future. Memories flooded back into Robi's mind, and he marveled at how things had come around for him and Gayatri—it was incredible and surreal.

During the final leg of her journey from Seoul, Gayatri managed to get some sleep. She noticed a few single women traveling with her, mostly air hostesses. She was awestruck by the service and lively interaction of the pleasant crew members. Feeling a bit lonely and overwhelmed by the travel logistics, she found the experience refreshing but couldn't help feeling homesick.

Thoughts of her childhood, parents, growing up with Abhi, and fondness shown by her grandparents, Abhi's parents, and friends inundated her with emotions. Tears welled up in her beautiful eyes, but she found solace in knowing that Robi would be waiting for her on the other side of the world.

The landing at SFO was smooth, and the crew members quickly prepared for the arrival process. Gayatri was impressed by the behavior of her fellow passengers throughout the journey. It was certainly a pleasant experience traveling along with them.

Robi couldn't contain his excitement while waiting at the reception area. Like many others, he held a large bouquet of roses in one hand and a cute teddy bear with "GAIROB" emblazoned on it and surrounded by a love sign. Glancing at the display board, he noticed that the SIA flight from Singapore via Seoul had arrived a little ahead of time. Passengers started coming out of the large double doors near the reception area, and amidst the hugs, cheers, crying, and camera flashes, Robi eagerly searched for the one he had been waiting for. He tried to remain patient, and didn't want anxiety to get the better of him.

Gracefully stepping down from the airplane onto the ramp with her hand-carry suitcase and handbag, Gayatri attracted attention with her grace and beauty. Gayatri smiled as she never expected to garner this kind of attention in a place like San Francisco.

She reveled in the atmosphere and the silent attention she received during the five-minute walk to the immigration area. Gayatri was enthralled by the methodical way passengers were ushered through the counter. A woman in uniform asked if she was a citizen or permanent resident, to which she replied neither and was promptly directed to the line for tourists and other visa holders.

While waiting in line, Gayatri wondered where exactly Robi would be waiting. Anxious to meet him, these additional few minutes felt like an eternity.

At the immigration counter, a jovial officer asked for her passport and visa papers. "Headed to Berkeley, young lady?" the officer asked in a soft tone.

"Yes, Sir, to the university!" Gayatri replied confidently.

The officer responded, "Wow, I was thinking you were headed to a beauty pageant contest, lady! By the way, that's a compliment!"

Gayatri thanked him, and as he stamped her passport, he said, "Well, you must be very smart as well going to Berkeley! Good luck with your stay here, and I presume you'll head back to your country upon graduation."

"Well, I think so Sir," Gayatri replied with a nice smile, while silently thinking to herself that she was in love with an American waiting outside and it all depended on him.

"Go ahead, all the best!" the officer said, parting with a gentle smirk.

Gayatri quickly proceeded to the baggage claim area, where she located her two bags, loaded them onto a trolley, and made her way to the customs area. After answering a couple of questions, she was waved through to the double-door exit area.

Seeing the "Welcome to San Francisco" sign, Gayatri felt a surge of exhilaration. Meanwhile, Robi focused on the double doors, and when he spotted the ravishing beauty with long hair pushing a trolley out, his entire body surged with excitement. It felt like a fairytale as he received Gayatri and hugged her tightly for a full minute. Equally excited, Gayatri blurted out, "Oh, I missed you so much, Robi."

"Welcome to America, baby! You look stunning, man! I am super excited to see you and hold you tight!" Robi exclaimed, handing her the bouquet and teddy bear while taking charge of the trolley.

Robi allowed Gayatri to settle down and take in the vibes of the new place. Speechless for a few minutes, she finally said, "I'm so happy to be here, Robi. I just can't believe it. I made it! To be with you."

"Oh, okay. No Berkeley then!" Robi teased with a big laugh.

"Very funny, kiddo! I'm going to get busy with my studies. So, not sure how much time..." Gayatri began, but Robi interrupted her, carrying her like a baby while joy and laughter permeated the air as some people cheered gently from the other side.

"You're possessive already, my dear prince!" Gayatri said, winking and giving him a mesmerizing smile.

"Nobody's going to blame me for that, baby. Well, I missed you. My parents are coming down to see you in Berkeley in a few days. They adore you, Gai," Robi said affectionately.

"I look forward to meeting them and all your friends, Mr. Robi!" Gayatri replied with a radiant smile.

The lovebirds drove onto Highway 101 and then onto the Bay Bridge towards Berkeley. Gayatri was mesmerized by the scenic beauty and the grandeur of everything—the roads, the cars, and the people. Jet lag and a bit of homesickness slowly crept in, but she was tremendously happy and excited to be back with Robi in his own backyard. She had pulled it off, and Robi called it a dream come true.

Settling down in Berkeley was a breeze for Gayatri, with Robi's frequent assistance in setting up her place and treating her to romantic dates at the finest restaurants in Berkeley and San Francisco. They were both thoroughly enjoying their time together, and Robi had already made plans for them to visit his parents in Santa Monica for Thanksgiving. Gayatri eagerly agreed and looked forward to the trip.

Gayatri quickly made friends on campus and was delighted to have Roma from Brazil as her roommate. They bonded over shopping and cooking, treating Robi to a delightful blend of Indian and Brazilian cuisine. They also relished their time attending parties in the dorm and other places on campus.

Despite being far from home, Gayatri managed her homesickness better than expected. She frequently called her parents and Abhi, finding solace and support in their conversations. She shared photos and videos with her loved ones, receiving updates from them in return. Life in Berkeley felt incredibly fulfilling, but she couldn't help but miss her home dearly.

Gayatri found the MBA coursework intense and noticed the brilliance of her classmates. The classroom sessions were highly interactive, with professors who were casual yet insightful in their teaching and assignments. Initially worried about falling behind, Gayatri's quick learning abilities allowed her to catch up and excel in all the subjects. She particularly enjoyed working in teams and making project presentations, finding it a refreshing change from the more monotonous approach she had experienced in Indian colleges.

The first semester flew by for Gayatri at a frenetic pace. Robi continued to visit her in Berkeley, introducing himself to her friends as her boyfriend. Gayatri's roommate, Roma, often described Robi as a tall, handsome hero straight out of romance novels, which never failed to make Gayatri blush.

Feeling the need for a break from their hectic routines, both Gayatri and Robi eagerly anticipated the Thanksgiving getaway. Robi had booked their flight tickets from Oakland to LA, and he picked her up from Berkeley to go to the airport. Gayatri thoroughly relished traveling with Robi, as he remained cool, jovial, and carefree throughout the journey.

During the short flight, Robi and Gayatri shared stories of their childhood travels with their parents, as well as their own adventures with friends. Curious again about Robi's lack of serious relationships before her, Gayatri asked him about it. Robi's answer remained consistent: he had never found the right person until Gayatri came into his life.

Robi wanted to ensure that Gayatri felt comfortable during her stay with his parents and meeting their close friends and relatives. As they walked out of the terminal exit, Gayatri was pleasantly surprised to be greeted by Robi's parents with bouquets and warm hugs. Gayatri playfully pinched Robi for pulling it off so smoothly. In addition to the warm welcome, the Bascoms had arranged for a limo to take them home.

Gayatri felt like she was in a fairyland as they drove to the beautiful Tudor-style home located in an upscale neighborhood. The well-manicured front yard, spacious driveway, and expansive backyard with a pool and spa were exactly as Abhi had described them years ago. The Bascoms ensured Gayatri's comfort in her new room, which had an attached bathroom and elegant furniture.

After indulging in an Italian-themed dinner of pasta, pizza, and Chianti, the Bascoms retired for the night, leaving Gayatri and Robi in the family room to watch TV together. Overwhelmed by the experience, Gayatri expressed her happiness to Robi, praising his amazing parents.

Robi replied, "They want us to cherish every moment after all we've been through. They will always be supportive, so get ready for more fun, baby! No major surprises, but we have a special Thanksgiving gathering with friends tomorrow and some sightseeing planned for the weekend."

The Thanksgiving party organized by the Bascoms, with Robi's assistance, was a resounding success. The pleasant weather allowed for cocktails and appetizers outdoors, followed by a turkey dinner buffet indoors. The Bascoms wanted their friends and a few close relatives in the area to meet Robi's girlfriend.

Gayatri looked stunning in an elegant red dress that exuded confidence and class. She became the center of attention, graciously accepting compliments from Robi's friends. One of Robi's college basketball teammates even remarked, "Robi is one lucky dude to have snagged someone like you!" Gayatri blushed and replied, "And do you think I haven't hit the jackpot with Robi? He's absolutely wonderful! Thank you for the sweet compliment!"

The party ended with everyone praising Gayatri for her courage and spirit. One of Robi's elderly neighbors emphatically said, "Live the American dream, my child!"

After a great Thanksgiving celebration and sightseeing in Los Angeles, Gayatri and Robi were ready to return to their respective homes in the Bay Area. They bid an emotional farewell to the Bascoms at the airport and boarded the plane back to Oakland. During the short flight, Gayatri reflected on the immense love and warmth she had received from Robi's family and the party attendees. She felt truly blessed and imagined a lifetime of companionship with Robi.

Chapter 30

Starting Strong: A Year of Promise

The year 2011 proved to be momentous for Gayatri and Robi. Both were busy with their respective college and work commitments. The first significant event came when Robi surprised everyone with the announcement that Abhi would be returning to the Bay Area. GOLI had been acquired by Robi's company, resulting in an easy and amicable acquisition for both parties. Abhi was delighted to get back to the Bay Area, this time accompanied by Janani.

This news was another dream come true for Gayatri. She was overjoyed that her beloved cousin brother Abhi and his wife would now be living close to her. Coinciding with Abhi and Janani's move, Gayatri completed her first year at Berkeley. They all decided to be in the East Bay to maintain close proximity. Furthermore, Gayatri secured a summer internship at Google, which added to her excitement.

On Abhi and Janani's arrival at SFO airport, Robi and Gayatri warmly received them. "Life has come full circle, dude," Robi said to Abhi.

Gayatri, feeling emotional, said tearfully, "So happy to have you both here."

Janani couldn't hold back her emotions and exclaimed, "Missed you badly, Gai..."

"Well, it's time to party like crazy, guys. Back to the good old days, but with a twist – we are hooked!" Abhi exclaimed with a naughty smirk.

The new arrivals were taken to a business apartment arranged by the company. Robi and Gayatri had already stocked the fridge and ordered Chinese and Thai food from local restaurants on Castro Street to kick off the celebration.

Janani was thrilled by the luxurious beginning in the Bay Area, grateful for what Robi had done for them.

While Abhi and Robi soaked in the moment, Gayatri bombarded them with questions, her excitement overflowing. Eventually, Robi interrupted with a big smile and said, "Well, ladies, can we start dinner now and continue our conversation while eating?"

"Of course, dear. We're ready! You'll love Thai food. Remember the luncheon at your favorite Thai place, 'Benjarong,' in Chennai, Abhi?" Gayatri asked.

Abhi chimed in with a massive smile, "How can I forget that, Gai! That was when Robi started hitting on you."

Laughter filled the air, followed by enthusiastic high fives.

After a satisfying meal and some ice cream, Robi and Gayatri bid farewell to Abhi and Janani, leaving them to take some rest after their long journey.

It was a great beginning for Abhi as he embarked on a new career in the Bay Area, now part of Robi's company. Though GOLI's acquisition was modest, it received significant attention, and Abhi was enthusiastic about all the developments. As part of the deal, both Goks and Anoop were offered positions in Mountain View to work for the new company.

After completing her two-month internship at Google, Gayatri focused on completing her coursework and project report. Thankfully, her professor allowed her to incorporate the work she had done during her internship, providing a valuable boost to her project on Business Analytics. She made sure she was well-prepared for job placement, with Abhi and Robi generously assisting her in resume preparation, job leads, and interview tips.

Gayatri, having gained confidence and knowledge during her time at Google, felt well-prepared for the intense job placement interviews. She had learned something new every day at the company and was ready to tackle any challenging question.

Gayatri and Robi frequently met in the Bay Area, often at Abhi's apartment in the East Bay. The location allowed them to explore various places of interest easily. Together, they toured important locations, from Napa to San Francisco to Santa Cruz, as well as key scenic spots along the Pacific Highway. The four of them enjoyed cycling and hiking, relishing the scenic views while getting a fantastic workout.

Gayatri found it hard to believe how quickly the fall semester was passing, filled with numerous interesting activities on campus. Thanksgiving was just a few days away, and plans had to be made once again.

Robi surprised everyone by booking a cruise trip to the Bahamas for all four of them. He declared it as a treat for them, although Abhi suspected there might be more surprises in store, as Robi was being coy about the details. All four eagerly anticipated the delightful cruise experience, as none of them had been on a cruise before.

The week leading up to Thanksgiving was spent packing and preparing for their cruise trip via Miami. Robi had reserved two special suites on the cruise liner. Excitement filled the air as they eagerly anticipated the adventures that awaited them.

Chapter 31

An Oceanic Escapade to the Bahamas

The flight from San Francisco to Miami felt long, but the four of them were chatting as if they hadn't seen each other in years. Robi built up the excitement about the cruise and their trip to the exotic Bahamas. Gayatri couldn't believe how their lives have been transformed, and the prospect of being on an elegant cruise in the Atlantic Ocean thrilled her.

Gayatri complimented Robi on his creative trip planning, and he replied with a sly smile and a hug, saying they were all going to have the time of their lives. As the plane touched down in Miami, the weary travelers were relieved to disembark and head to the Miami harbor, where the cruise liner awaited them. A short cab ride took them to the harbor, where they joined the line of colorfully dressed tourists eager to board the ship.

For Janani and Gayatri, the concept of a cruise liner was completely new. The ship resembled a magnificent five-star hotel. Janani couldn't contain her excitement and exclaimed how amazing everything was, thanking Robi profusely for making it all happen. Robi explained that the cruise offered free food and entertainment, with charges only for drinks and onboard purchases.

Amidst light-hearted jokes and banter, the captain's horn sounded, signaling the last call for boarding. Laughter and photo-taking filled the air as the four friends joined the other passengers in boarding the ship. They swiftly checked into their suites, and another siren marked the ship's readiness to set sail. The captain welcomed everyone over the PA system and reminded them to read and follow the safety instructions.

After a quick refresh and change of clothes, the inseparable group of four felt a sense of relief and freedom as they leisurely strolled around the deck, dressed in shorts and sandals. The ocean view and the ship cutting through the water created a paradise-like atmosphere, and everyone seemed to revel in the experience.

Robi called the others aside and instructed them to dress formally for dinner. He had arranged a special table on the upper deck, promising exclusive service and a five-course meal accompanied by champagne and cocktails. Excitement filled the air as they anticipated the luxurious dining experience.

After soaking in the evening sunset for an hour, the friends returned to their suites to get ready for dinner. They agreed to meet on the upper deck in approximately 30 minutes.

Gayatri wore a classy blue dress with a matching pearl necklace adoring her lovely neck. The snug-fitting designer dress and high-heeled shoes made her stand out like a supermodel. Robi was speechless for a moment when he saw her and could not help saying, "You are so incredibly beautiful! What a classic beauty, babe! You are going to make a lot of heads turn!"

"Oh, you have become really possessive, my man! This is the designer dress you gifted me and the pearl necklace was given by my parents. Glad you like it so much!" said Gayatri.

"Like it? I just love it! You look super marvelous! Let us get out and enjoy, Babe," said Robi while pulling her out of the suite onto the deck.

Robi also wore the best outfit he had carried for the occasion. He was excited to the core and his heart was pounding as he held Gayatri in his arms and gently strolled over to the upper deck. Janani and Abhi were already there and exclaimed in unison, "Wow, look at that! What a gorgeous couple!"

"You guys look stunning. That is such a classy outfit, Gai. Looks great on you," said Janani with no pretense.

"Well, Robi, you've turned my sister into a supermodel, dude!" said Abhi.

"See, I told you, Gai. I am not the only one who thinks you are a supermodel!" added Robi.

The setting in the blue ocean was perfect. The gentle breeze and sound of waves were soothing to all the holiday goers. The exclusive table setting was even more splendid filled with chrysanthemums and roses and a glowing candlelight in the middle.

Robi said that he had pre-ordered the food to make it easy on everyone. He asked Charlie, the waiter, dressed in a tux to bring the champagne and serve them. There would be no compromise for this occasion. Charlie brought the best Champagne Dom Perignon in a silver ice bowl along with four glasses.

Gayatri was excited and brimming with joy. She was holding Robi's hand tightly and also noticed Robi sweating a bit and breathing heavily. "Are you okay, Robi? I have never seen you panting all of a sudden?" She took out a soft tissue from her handbag and started wiping his forehead and neck. Abhi and Janani were all smiles.

"Don't worry, sweetheart. I am just over-excited. Let us have the champagne," said Robi. He gently raised the glass and got up from his chair. "Well, before I say cheers, I want to thank you all for joining me on this journey… which is actually just beginning, in my opinion."

Robi was ready to pull off the surprise now. Choked by emotions, Robi took out a small blue box from his pocket, went down on his knees in front of Gai, and asked her, "Gai, you are the love of my life, my only one. Will you marry me?"

Abhi and Janani were speechless and unable to control their emotions as well.

Gayatri felt a surge of emotions taking over her while she exclaimed, "Oh my God, Robi! This is too much! Are you sure, baby?"

Her eyes began to well up with uncontrollable tears.

Robi did not say anything but just moved his head up and down while clearing up his throat.

"I will, I sure will, Robi. You are my man!" cried Gayatri while hugging him and allowing him to put the lovely solitaire purchased by his mother on her left ring finger. It was a dream come true for both of them and the couple hugged for a good two minutes oblivious of the fact that many around the upper deck were watching the lovely scene and applauding.

Janani and Abhi hugged and congratulated them. "This is a massive surprise, dude! Only you can pull off something like this. So, happy for both of you. Congratulations!"

Gayatri was still emotional and could not take her eyes off the diamond ring. "This is too much, Robi! I love it!"

"You know my mom, babe. She helped me pick the finest one from Tiffany's. This is just the beginning, sweetheart," said Robi in a highly ecstatic mood.

Finally, Abhi got up with his champagne glass to raise a toast. "For my dear, Gai and Robi! You guys truly deserve each other.

I am immensely thrilled and cannot wait to be your best man at the wedding. Cheers! Love you, guys!"

Gayatri started to get more emotional and so did Janani. All of them hugged and shed tears of joy, soaking in the moment. "I cannot wait for the wedding day either. So happy for the two of you. Love you, guys!" said Janani in a quivering voice.

In yet another surprise, Robi held Gayatri in her arms and did an honor lap around the deck while everyone cheered and congratulated them.

Gayatri was on cloud nine. She just could not believe what was happening. Abhi and Janani were too happy taking photos and recording the event. They were relishing in the moment and did not expect Robi to pull off such a huge surprise so gracefully.

It took almost 45 minutes for Gai and Robi to get back to square one and resume the dinner. Gayatri was still in a daze when the soup and salads were being served. Robi had to feed her the salad while she was sampling the soup in a state of newfound ecstasy.

However, she was back in her element when her favorite seafood platter was served. She decided to enjoy every bit of it while feeding Robi who was now nibbling his food.

"C'mon, guys! Time to savor your lovely dinner and get back to more celebrations!' said Abhi with a big smile and nudging Janani.

The live music group started playing all the celebratory songs as requested by the chief of staff. The captain came over and handed a bouquet of flowers, while the cake was set up on the table for the newly engaged couple. It was all well-orchestrated and Gayatri was speechless again, but reveling in the moment. They cut the lovely chocolate cake that had all the fancy decorations and a message: *"Congratulations GAIROB"* neatly embossed. Gayatri took the lead in taking a small piece and pasting it all over Robi's face, while he gently made her sit on his lap and fed her the cake. Gayatri then served the cake to Abhi and Janani who were all smiles and brimming in total happiness.

Robi requested the deck staff to serve the cake to all the patrons in the upper deck and ordered a round of cocktails for all. Robi wanted to share his happiness with everyone. He was in a different frame of mind altogether. The angelic Gayatri had a phenomenal and positive effect on him.

Robi just wanted to dance with Gayatri all night. For the slow, romantic melodies, he was holding Gayatri tight and lifting her to touch the ceiling between each song. Janani and Abhi joined the dance floor for the slow dance. It was just a spectacular night for all four of them. They never dreamed of such an experience!

Gayatri would not let go of Robi as they reached the suite past midnight. In an ecstatic mood she spoke softly, "What are you waiting for, my prince? We are officially engaged! Let's cuddle up baby!"

With a surge of excitement, Robi gently carried Gayatri to bed, and in no time, were engrossed in intimate cuddling. The bond was now complete.

The wait had been worth it for both of them, and as they embraced the moment, Gayatri and Robi knew their journey together had just begun.

The short trip to the Bahamas was a whirlwind of fun, surprise and romance. The lovebirds, Gayatri and Robi, captured countless snapshots, their exhilaration evident in their faces. They explored the Bahamas alongside other young tourists, immersing themselves in the local cuisine, trying out different beers, and indulging in some shopping. The experience was incredibly relaxing, making it difficult to say goodbye, but they knew the time had come to board the ship back to Miami.

Gayatri hugged Robi tightly, feeling a profuse urge to share her incredible cruise experience with her parents, uncle, aunt, and all her friends. She couldn't contain her elation about becoming Mrs. Gayatri Bascom soon and was eager to announce it to the world. In that moment, Gayatri was completely absorbed in her happiness, and Robi couldn't help but smile as he watched her dreamy state.

Chuckling, Gayatri playfully pushed Robi to the other side of the couch, teasing him about the attention they would receive. "I'm going to be busy letting everyone know as to how you snagged me, baby," she said with a laugh.

Robi joined in the fun, wrapping his arms around Gayatri and pulling her closer. "Well, go for it, you own me now baby!" he replied, a mischievous glint in his eyes.

Feeling a sense of fulfillment, Gayatri pleaded with Robi to start planning their future together, involving both sets of parents. She wanted to ensure that everyone was happy and involved in their journey. Robi agreed wholeheartedly, emphasizing the importance of surrounding themselves with joyous people. They decided to set the wedding dates for July or August next year, after Gayatri completed her studies.

Gayatri expressed her enthusiasm for the plan, acknowledging that it would allow them ample time to organize events in both Los Angeles and Chennai.

Robi playfully mentioned "Chennai again, oh no!" causing Gayatri to throw a pillow at him. They bantered back and forth, with Gayatri referring to him as "Chennai Mappillai".

Curious, Robi asked Gayatri about the meaning of "Mappillai." Gayatri reminded him jovially that he needed to learn the lingo as a soon-to-be son-in-law of Chennai. They shared a joyous moment, their love and laughter filling the air.

As the ship gently sailed in the Atlantic, the love smitten couple found solace in each other's arms, exhausted from their momentous escapade. They drifted off to sleep, cherishing the heavenly experience they had shared with their dear friends, Abhi and Janani. Although it felt too short, they acknowledged that it was time to return to their regular routines, carrying the memories of their incredible journey with them.

Chapter 32

A Bountiful Yield

The 2011 Christmas holiday season was a busy time for everyone. Gayatri had to work until the last day of the semester to complete numerous assignments. She was relieved that the coursework was over, and she only had a few months left to finish her project work for her MBA course. In a stroke of good fortune, Gayatri was offered an excellent entry-level position as a business analyst at Google. Her impressive performance during her internship led to a short and informal interview, and she received the offer letter the same day.

Robi and Abhi returned from their trip to Asia Pacific just in time for the holidays, while Janani kept herself occupied with certification courses at Santa Clara University. The four of them decided to relax and focus on planning the wedding during the holiday season.

Gayatri waited for the right moment to share the news about her job offer with Google, which would place her close to Robi's workplace. She invited Robi's parents for the Christmas weekend and chose that occasion to announce her new job. The announcement was met with hugs and high fives, filling the air with joy.

Everything seemed to fall into place for Gayatri. Overwhelmed with gratitude, she began sharing the news of her professional journey at Google with her parents, relatives, and friends.

As the new year approached, Gayatri, Robi, and Abhi celebrated in style in San Francisco, exchanging wishes for an exciting year ahead. Gayatri eagerly looked forward to her MBA graduation, her new role at Google, and the grand wedding planned for that summer in LA and Chennai.

Gayatri's parents called her via Skype to wish her a happy new year and express their happiness about her new job in the Bay Area. They assured her that she had a promising future. Overwhelmed with emotion, Gayatri shed tears of joy. She requested her parents to be present for her graduation in June, and they eagerly agreed.

Gayatri also informed them about Robi's proposal to marry her. She categorically mentioned that she needed their approval and blessings for her to formalize everything. There was a long silence at the other end. Finally, her father surprised her "That's good news Gai. Amma and I only want you to be happy. How about the wedding dates?"

Taken aback and with tears of joy flowing down her cheeks, Gayatri shared her plans for a simple wedding and reception in LA while having the Muhurtham and a grand reception in Chennai the following month. Her parents enthusiastically offered to take care of the arrangements in Chennai and eagerly awaited the dates.

"Thank you so much Amma and Appa! I have unknowingly hurt your feelings and became a bit self-centered! Sorry! I did not mean too…" sobbed Gayatri incessantly.

"We are also at fault Gai! We know the world is changing. And, we know that you will only do the right things. Do not worry. It is all water under the bridge" said Gayatri's dad in an affectionate tone.

"I know you will always be on my side Appa and Amma!" said Gayatri.

"I regret my actions, Gai. Please convey my apologies to Robi and his parents. I wish I had handled the situation with decorum and dignity. I now realize that I cannot be possessive and dictate terms. You are grown up, smart and know what you are doing."

"Also, Gai, I met my long-time college friend, Arunkumar Paul, whose daughter has settled down now in Australia, and has gotten married to a doctor of Kenyan origin. He is so happy about his daughter's choice after having had some initial reservations. Arunkumar is a proud grandfather now. I am sure you will make me very proud Gai!"

"That's so sweet Appa. Yes, I will make you and Amma proud! Always!"

Gayatri's heart ached with longing and love as she expressed her desire to see her parents. She missed them dearly, but found solace in their support and reassurance that they wanted to see her happy.

Charged with renewed energy and happiness, Gayatri focused on completing her project and wrapping it up. The task of typing up the project report and preparing for the review felt overwhelming, but she was determined to finish the last lap in style. She completed her project ahead of time and submitted it.

The spring season of 2012 brought a renewed sense of cheer to the campus, particularly for those graduating and entering the real world. Gayatri and Roma found themselves reminiscing about how quickly events had unfolded on campus, still feeling a sense of disbelief.

Robi suggested that Gayatri move in with him since she had very little work on campus. Gayatri agreed, seeing the benefits of living together in terms of planning the weddings in two different locations, as well as her graduation and subsequent celebrations.

Robi and his father organized the date for the church wedding in LA and the reception at a nearby Marriott Hotel. Robi's parents insisted on covering the reception expenses, while Robi took care of the church wedding expenses. The Bascoms wanted it to be an extraordinary event for their only son and their lovely daughter-in-law.

The Bascoms, Gayatri, and Abhi finalized the LA wedding date and guest list, setting the process in motion. It was scheduled for exactly two weeks after Gayatri's graduation. The Muhurtham and reception in Chennai were set to take place at The Grand Chola in August, fully organized and funded by Gayatri's parents.

It was yet another time to go to the SFO airport. This time it was an entourage comprising of Gayatri, Abhi, Robi and Janani to receive the parents of Gayatri and Abhi traveling from India.

The weary travelers arrived on time and came through the large entry door to the reception area. It was emotional déjà vu all over again. Gayatri could not hold back her tears while hugging her parents, uncle and aunt. Robi graciously embraced and welcomed both sets of parents with bouquets. Abhi and Janani were speechless witnessing the beautiful scene unfolding before them. It was a massive turn of events for the entire family, especially Gayatri and Robi.

It was time to get the well-deserved celebrations into full gear!

On the morning of her graduation day at UC Berkeley, Gayatri was swept away by emotions. She also looked forward to the party at Fairmont Hotel in San Francisco. Everything seemed to be happening in a whirlwind for Gayatri.

In a surprise move, Abhi announced that he would cover the entire bill for the graduation party at the Fairmont Hotel, which included about 100 guests. Despite protests from both Robi and Gayatri, Abhi insisted it was his treat and no going back. They headed to the ceremony hall, ready to cherish every moment of the graduation ceremony.

As expected, Gayatri was the center of attention at both the graduation ceremony and the party. Her parents shed tears of joy, visibly proud of their daughter's accomplishments. They had replaced their initial apprehension and societal pressures with pure happiness, positive energy, and blessings for their daughter and future son-in-law. They deeply regretted again putting them through unnecessary hardships and failing to adapt to the changing times.

Abhi and Robi ensured that there were plenty of photos taken and hugs shared, making it a memorable experience for Gayatri. Abhi spared no expense for the party, even arranging a DJ to play Indian beats for the dancing session.

Robi proudly showed off his beautiful fiancée, basking in the joy of having the love of his life celebrate her graduation from a prestigious university and securing a position at Google.

Robi's parents competed with him to introduce Gayatri to everyone they knew, spreading big smiles and laughter wherever they went. Gayatri's parents, along with Kumar and Malini, joined in, meeting all the well-wishers and inviting them to the next momentous event—the wedding of Robi and Gayatri—in a traditional Indian style in August.

After the long graduation ceremony and vibrant party, Robi and Gayatri were completely exhausted. Gayatri thoroughly enjoyed meeting all the people and was amazed by the vibrant atmosphere at the Fairmont Party Hall. Abhi's generosity in throwing such a grand party, complete with delicious seafood, and the perfect DJ music put her on an emotional high.

Robi and Gayatri hugged each other tightly, succumbing to exhaustion as they drifted off to sleep.

Chapter 33

GAIROB: Moment of Tango

Both Robi and Abhi had taken some time off from work to prepare for the wedding in Santa Monica, California. They had sent out about 200 invitations, and more than 90% had confirmed their presence at the wedding and reception. Despite having an event management company handling all the details, the Bascoms, along with Gayatri and Abhi, had to oversee many things, including a quick wedding rehearsal orchestrated by Maggie and her friends.

As part of the rehearsal, Gayatri had to try on her magnificent white wedding gown, which was purchased by the Bascoms, and the exquisite diamond necklace brought from India by her parents. Most of all, Gayatri rejoiced in practicing the walk with her father to the church podium.

The big day finally arrived—the day both Robi and Gayatri had been waiting for! It was a nervous morning for both of them as they checked on a lot of things. Abhi and Janani were looking into every single detail with the event management company. Roma and Janani helped Gayatri with her makeup and dressing, while Abhi stayed with Robi to ensure that his tuxedo dressing went smoothly. The radiant couple and the family entourage were decked out and ready to go in their respective limousines.

Robi and Abhi left in the limo along with their parents. Robi reminisced about the ride in Chennai with Abhi to the wedding hall about three years back. The Kumars were filled with excitement to be a part of an event that was expected to be transcendent. The Bascoms were in high spirits and decided to savor every moment.

The setting was perfect—lovely sunshine, light traffic, and lush greenery along the route the limo was taking. The church was bustling with energy like never before, with people in formal attire walking gently to their seats in the church's main hall. The camera crew, music ensemble, flower girls, and ushers were all working professionally to make it one of the most eventful and memorable occasions for the lovely couple.

The Bascoms, along with the Kumars, walked in, breaking the hushed silence in the church. They were greeted by all the guests who had already filled every seat. There were hugs galore and whistles from Robi's childhood friends as the two handsome men—Robi and his best man Abhi—made their way down the aisle to the main podium area. The music ensemble played a couple of tunes to liven up the environment while waiting for the bride to arrive.

At exactly 5:00 PM, the limo carrying the bride, the bridesmaids Janani and Roma, and the Ranjans pulled into the elegant church driveway. The parents got down first and helped Gayatri, who was wearing an ultra-gorgeous wedding gown and classy makeup, adorned with a shining diamond necklace and perfectly matching high heel shoes, to exit the limo. The bridesmaids helped Gayatri hold her gown in place as she gracefully walked to the entrance.

The moment arrived, and the music, "Here comes the bride," filled the hall in a melodious manner, welcoming Gayatri as her father elegantly walked her up to the altar. The well-dressed bridesmaids followed the bride and father. Gayatri stepped onto the podium to be received by the groom. They were all smiles as the bride and groom stood at the altar, facing each other.

The guests in the audience ran out of adjectives to describe the absolutely stunning couple standing graciously in front of the pastor to take their wedding vows. The main elders—Bascoms, Ranjans, and Kumars—were in tears but smiling and holding hands together.

The formalities started with the pastor jokingly saying to the bride, "I have known this guy for many years. Are you sure?" with a big mischievous smile.

Gayatri playfully retorted, "Well, it's too late for that now!"

"There you go, child," said the pastor with a gentle smile and a wink at Robi.

He then began the proceedings after reading a few verses from the Bible.

"Robinson Ebenezar Bascom, do you take Gayatri Ranjan as your lawfully wedded wife?" the pastor asked.

Robi smiled and replied, "I do."

"And you, Gayatri Ranjan, do you take Robinson Ebenezar Bascom as your lawfully wedded husband?"

"I do," said Gayatri, bringing loud cheers from the audience.

"Great! In the name of the Lord, I declare you Man and Wife. God Bless Mrs. and Mr. Robi Bascom!"

The room erupted with applause. The newlyweds were overwhelmed as they gazed upon the sea of smiling faces.

"Okay then, Robi, you may now kiss the bride!"

Robi placed a passionate kiss on Gayatri's lips as camera flashes went off all around and the audience erupted in rapturous applause, which lasted for a full two minutes. The elders hugged each other first, and then the well-wishers in the audience rushed

to congratulate the Bascoms and Ranjans. The newlyweds walked
down the aisle gracefully, holding each other's hand, to the exit for
the final formalities.

The audience marched out in unison and headed to the Marriott
Ballroom for the most awaited reception arranged by the Bascoms.
The reception started on time, and all the guests were seated and
served delectable cocktails. The newlywed couple sat at the front
with their respective parents, Janani and their best man, savoring
the dinner and preparing for the toasts and dancing. Among the
invited guests were Goks and Anoop, appreciating every moment
of the proceedings!

The Bascoms went to great lengths to ensure that a five-
course meal was served to the guests, while the Jazz band played
melodious music in tune with the occasion.

The evening's MC—a close friend of the Bascoms and a
former cable TV show host—took the mic and walked around,
calling for everyone's attention.

"Hi everyone! Are you ready? ARE YOU READY to celebrate?
I hope you all had enough cocktails to drown in this spectacular
occasion! Oh, what a catch, Robi! You have snatched one of the
most gorgeous women on the planet, bro!"

Laughter filled the packed ballroom. "You broke the hearts of
half a billion men in India, dude. And some of us here as well."
Massive laughter followed by some gentle teasing, all aimed at the
handsome bridegroom.

"Okay, folks! I am so happy for the Bascoms and the Ranjans.
And you, Gai, you can't change your mind now!" The room roared
with cheers and applause.

"Before we get to the cake-cutting and ceremonial dance, let me invite the best man, Abhi, to do the toast and the roast!"

Abhi, adorned in his classy tuxedo, accepted the mic from the MC and spoke extemporaneously with great elan:

"Well, Robi, I invited you to India a couple of years ago to be at my wedding and enjoy the Indian adventure. But you went on an adventure of your own, and took away my sister as well!" he said, pointing to Gayatri with a playful chuckle.

A voice from the audience joined in, "You are the man, Abhi! Thought you had a shotgun, dude, to protect Gai!"

Abhi laughed and moved around elegantly, engrossed in the moment.

"Alright, guys, too late for that now! Ughh, anyway, it's amazing to see how destiny has connected the dots so well for us, Robi... You and me at Stanford, Gai and you in Chennai, and all of us here in California. It's just wonderful to think about how love has transformed and transfixed us all in a whirlwind manner."

I have to say this, folks... The effect that Gai and Robi have on each other is something out of this world, beyond any bland, run-of-the-mill storybook stuff. This is romance at a global level, traversing continents. The powerful embodiment of love kept them glued together and made them overcome many obstacles that came their way. The grit and commitment shown by both of them are to be emulated by generations to come."

True love prevailed here, not societal pressure.

"Real victory and happiness are obtained only when two lovely beings tango together in unison, without missing a beat—such is your synergy, my dear Robi and Gai."

"Now, let's all raise our glasses to this lovely, made-for-each-other couple! Here's to both of you, wishing you total bliss! Enjoy every moment, guys! Cheers!"

Everyone raised their glasses, cheering for the young couple. While Gayatri shed tears of joy, Robi stood up to hug Abhi, and everyone in the audience gave them a rousing ovation that was emotional for the Bascoms, Ranjans, and Kumars.

The MC returned. "Well, that was short and sweet, yet truly heartfelt. What a guy! What emotions! Thank you, Abhi."

The evening became more boisterous as expected, with lots of exotic cocktails, dancing, merriment, and an abundance of hugs. Every soul in the ballroom was completely immersed in the grandeur of the celebrations.

The grand finale and emotional highlight came when Gayatri and her father performed the traditional 'on the heels' dance, with everyone cheering them on!

The Bascoms were immensely happy that so many people graced the occasion and made the lovely couple even more ecstatic, creating awesome moments to cherish forever.

Chapter 34

"Take Me Back to the Start"

After a blissful honeymoon in Mexico, Gayatri and Robi returned to the Bay Area, ready to embark on the second part of their marital journey—the big, fat Indian wedding in *Singara* Chennai.

As they arrived at the Chennai International Airport, they were greeted by a large entourage of people. Stepping onto the familiar land that had transformed Robi's life, he felt a sense of triumph despite the emotional ups and downs he had experienced. Robi was determined to savor every moment of this occasion.

The Ranjans had arrived a few days earlier to make all the necessary wedding arrangements at the Grand Chola Hotel. Indian weddings are known for their opulence, and although Gayatri and her parents had decided to compress all the events into a single day, the preparations were still extensive.

At the airport reception area, Robi hugged and lifted driver Vetri, showing his affection and gratitude. "We made it, Vetri Bro! You asked me to come back, and here I am!"

Gayatri, holding back tears, patted Vetri affectionately and said, "Thank you Vetri *Anna*!". Vetri was speechless and in tears as well.

While the rest of the US contingent checked into the premier rooms at the Grand Chola Hotel, Gayatri chose to stay with her parents to assist with the preparations.

The wedding day commenced with the traditional Muhurtham ceremony held in a specially decorated ballroom. The Ranjans had planned a compact yet meaningful ceremony that incorporated all the important rituals.

As a mark of tradition, the Ranjans presented Robi with a silk dhoti, a silk shirt, and a gold Omega watch. Robi graciously accepted the gifts, expressing his heartfelt gratitude and embracing them. Abhi, being the best man, assisted Robi in getting dressed in the exquisite silk attire.

"We'll start the ceremony in a few minutes, Robi. I'm sure you'll be comfortable in the new outfit," Ranjan said with a mischievous smile.

Robi was thrilled to don the finely tailored silk attire. He couldn't help but ask, "But why the gold watch, Abhi?"

"That's the dowry, man! Along with the watch, you also get 56 kg of Gai in pure 24-carat gold," Abhi replied jokingly.

Robi chuckled and replied, overcome with emotion, "Oh man, that's the best line I've heard so far! It's a bit too much, but I'm going to cherish this watch forever, along with the other 56 kg you mentioned."

Abhi smiled and said, "Sounds good, Robi! You look dapper in that Mappillai outfit, man. Let's go and rejoice in the Muhurtham rituals. Just follow along and repeat what the priest asks you to say, okay?"

"I'm going to do what you did at your wedding, Abhi. I still remember that stuff," Robi replied confidently.

Dressed in traditional Tamilian attire, the two handsome men walked to the main arena accompanied by a group of friends adorned in equally vibrant clothing. The playing of traditional Muhurtham music added to the festive atmosphere.

Robi took his seat on a small wooden stool inside the beautifully decorated pandal, with Abhi by his side. The surroundings were adorned with vibrant colors and elegant decorations. The guests seated in the audience shimmered with colorful sarees and jewelry, making Robi realize the opulence of the occasion.

In a classy gesture, the Ranjans escorted the Bascoms to the main pandal area to be alongside the bride and groom during the ceremony. Robi's emotions intensified when he saw his parents dressed in traditional Indian attire. He was overjoyed that they were there to witness and partake in this momentous event.

Amidst the resounding music of the trombone and traditional percussion instruments, the bride, looking absolutely stunning in a radiant red sari and glittering jewelry, entered the pandal accompanied by her entourage.

Seated next to the bridegroom, Gayatri was assisted by Janani and her mother. Robi nudged Gayatri and whispered, "Woah! You look stunning, Babe!"

"You too, my man," Gayatri replied, signaling him to be quiet as the proceedings began.

The jovial priest guided Robi through the recitation of mantras, which Robi delivered with a charmingly convoluted accent, delighting the guests. The Bascoms proudly patted their son, expressing their approval.

"You should have prepped me on this stuff, Babe," Robi whispered to Gayatri.

"Well, that would have taken away the element of surprise, dear," Gayatri replied with a smile.

After completing all the customary rituals, the priest announced the highly anticipated moment—the 'Thali Ceremony". The silver plate with the sacred golden thread, Thali, on a fresh coconut was handed to the priest, who asked the elders to touch it as a sign of blessing.

With the traditional *"ketu melam"* beat resounding and Janani holding the ceremonial 'Kamakshi' lamp in the background, the priest instructed Robi to tie the sacred thali around the bride's neck. As the drum beat reached its crescendo, Robi elegantly fastened the thali around Gayatri's neck, and the crowd surged forward to shower their blessings on the newlywed couple. The culmination of the ceremony brought smiles and tears of joy to the parents and loved ones.

Robi was once again on cloud nine. The moment he had eagerly awaited had finally arrived. It was an indescribable feeling of happiness for both Gayatri and Robi.

After completing the remaining formalities, the couple walked hand in hand to the adjacent hall for a lavish lunch with their loved ones.

Following a short break, Robi and Gayatri prepared themselves for the grand cocktail reception scheduled a few hours later. They changed into different outfits—Robi in a fancy Sherwani and Gayatri in an exquisite Lehenga Choli—both selected by Janani and Abhi. The guests were requested to dress in fancy ethnic wear, including the Bascoms.

The Ranjans went all out to host an extravagant reception, featuring a buffet dinner and multiple bars serving cocktails to the guests. The musical entertainment included a classical music group for the traditional mixers, followed by a DJ for those who wanted to dance the night away.

Gayatri and Robi became the center of attention as they stood on the dais, greeting the numerous guests—there were at least a thousand in attendance. The Bascoms were in awe of the grandeur of the event, witnessing firsthand the magnificence of a big, fat Indian wedding.

The Ranjans spared no effort in ensuring their only child's happiness. They wanted nothing but sheer joy for their daughter and new son-in-law. Their outlook had taken a 180° turn, perhaps paving the way for the society to emulate.

As Gayatri and Robi boarded the flight back to SFO after the whirlwind events, Robi couldn't help but reflect on the extraordinary circumstances. "I'm one of those ultra-privileged guys who got married to the same person twice, Babe—within two weeks and in two different continents! Not sure which one is really valid, hahaha..." he laughed.

Gayatri smiled and replied, "Oh, that's funny, honey! I know you're going to brag about it to your friends, right?"

"Why not? I have a total beauty to show off," Robi replied playfully.

"Goodness me! That should put me to sound sleep now," said Gayatri, resting her head on Robi's shoulder and hugging him tightly.

As they disembarked from the flight at SFO, it felt like a familiar routine for Robi. Gayatri found it hard to believe that she was back in her adopted city, now married to the man she had come to adore so deeply. It was a dream come true, and they were immensely grateful to all the people who had made it possible.

Chapter 35

Yet Another Thanksgiving

Gayatri, Robi, Abhi, and Janani continued to spend a lot of time together in the Bay Area, despite their busy schedules and frequent travels. They made a conscious effort to hang out together and explore new places and experiences as a tight-knit group. Their bond grew stronger with each passing day.

In November, they gathered once again at the Bascom Mansion in Southern California to celebrate Thanksgiving. The tradition had become increasingly popular, attracting a larger crowd. Maggie and Malcolm, understanding the preferences of the younger ones, spared no effort in making the party extravagant and memorable.

During the Thanksgiving lunch, as everyone raised their glasses for a toast, Robi prodded Gayatri, encouraging her to share some news. With a coy smile, Gayatri announced, "Well, I have some exciting news to share. Robi has been a bit mischievous, and I am three months pregnant. We are expecting our little one in June!"

The announcement elicited an eruption of joy and cheers from everyone around the table. Abhi, overcome with happiness, boldly lifted Gayatri from her chair and showered her with kisses on her cheeks. Hugs, congratulations, and well wishes followed as the entire gathering celebrated the joyous news.

Abhi, still beaming with excitement, teasingly remarked to Robi, "That was some quick work, my friend! I'm tremendously thrilled for both of you!"

The pervasive joy in the room left Maggie speechless, and she noticed her husband discreetly wiping away tears of happiness. "We feel truly blessed," he finally managed to say.

"Thank you all so much for your love and support. The journey of joy continues, my friends," Robi graciously expressed, his words filled with elegance.

Robi then playfully turned the attention to Abhi and Janani, saying, "Now, we are waiting for you to do something, Abhi!"

Abhi, wearing a mischievous smile, responded, "Well, my friends, I am ready! Are you ready, Janani?"

Janani, with a hint of excitement, chimed in, "Oh, Abhi never lets me keep any secret! I must share that we are also expecting a baby around the same time!"

The revelation sent the room into even wilder cheers and screams of joy. Gayatri was astounded by the coincidence and immense happiness that filled the air.

Even Goks, who was mostly reserved, couldn't help but join in the celebration. Turning to Abhi and Robi, he jokingly asked, "Do you guys' plan everything together? Hehehe..."

"Hey, Goks! That's a good one, my friend. While we may not plan everything, we are beyond thrilled that things are falling into place for both of us. It's been truly a wild ride, and there is so much to celebrate and look forward to!" Robi responded, his voice filled with emotion.

Anoop, who had grown more confident since starting his relationship with Bethany from the same office, chimed in, "I would love to make a movie out of this incredible story, folks!"

Senior Bascom joined the conversation, saying, "Well, Anoop, I'll fund your movie project! Go for it, son!"

"Thank you, Sir! And I already have a name for it: 'Monsoon Tango!'" Anoop beamed confidently, receiving high fives from everyone.

In June, Gayatri gave birth to a baby boy at El Camino Hospital, while Janani gave birth to a baby girl at Stanford University Children's Hospital. The families were overjoyed and felt complete. The grandparents shuttled between the two hospitals, proudly showing off their adorable grandchildren to friends and well-wishers.

Friendships and love continued to flourish, and it was a fitting end to their incredible journey.

"All's well that ends well".

Epilogue

The GOLI Folks in 2023

The GOLI team's journey continued to unfold with remarkable achievements and exciting new chapters in their lives. Let's take a closer look at their exceptional endeavors after ten years:

Anoop tied the knot with his long-time partner, Bethany, after a decade of dating. They settled into a spacious home in Los Altos. Anoop's dedication and expertise earned him a well-deserved promotion as the head of the Engineering Group in the company that acquired GOLI.

Goks, on the other hand, returned to India to lead the operations of the same company. His wedding took place shortly before the global pandemic, and he found love in his colleague Swetha, who coincidentally shared his hometown roots.

Gayatri made a bold career move by resigning as VP of Business Operations at Google. She embarked on a new adventure, joining a prestigious venture capital firm on Sandhill Road. Balancing her professional aspirations and the joys of raising Robi Raj Jr., she fearlessly embraced the challenges that lay ahead.

Janani's entrepreneurial spirit thrived as she co-founded a highly successful healthcare consulting firm with her classmates. Managing the demands of her growing business and caring for her daughter, Meghna, she proved her tenacity and expertise in the field.

Both Abhi and Robi found success as angel investors, making strategic early-stage investments. Together, they made approximately 20 investments, including a pivotal stake in a security company that swiftly achieved unicorn status within three years.

Currently, Robi and Gayatri reside in a luxurious home in Atherton, CA, basking in the fruits of their labor. Meanwhile, Abhi and Janani discovered their own slice of paradise in the form of a charming mansion nestled in the Los Altos Hills.

The collective net worth of these six extraordinary individuals who made GOLI a reality has surpassed a billion dollars. To honor their success and give back to their homeland, they established the 'GOLI fund,' dedicated to supporting educational and entrepreneurial initiatives in India.

True to his promise, Anoop diligently wrote and published the book titled "Monsoon Tango." Inspired by their incredible journey, he aspires to transform it into a sensational blockbuster, envisioning its release on a popular OTT platform.

As their paths continue to unfold, the GOLI team stands as a testament to the power of friendship, determination, and unwavering ambition. Together, they have left an indelible mark on the world, forging a legacy that will inspire generations to come.